THE CANTABRIGIAN

ROWING SOCIETY'S

SATURDAY NIGHT BASH

and other stories

Also by Roger Lee Kenvin

Harpo's Garden, short stories, 1997

The Gaffer and Seven Fables, short stories, 1987

Krishnalight, a play, 1976

THE CANTABRIGIAN

ROWING SOCIETY'S

SATURDAY NIGHT BASH

and other stories

by

Roger Lee Kenvin

July Blue Press

Published by **July Blue Press**, 127 N. Madison Avenue, Suite 208-C, Pasadena, California, 91101. Tel: (626) 445-4420.

First printing 1998

Printed in the United States of America by Odyssey Press Inc., Dover, New Hampshire

Library of Congress Catalog Card Number: 97-73926

ISBN 0-9656635-1-5

ACKNOWLEDGMENT

"The Cantabrigian Rowing Society's Saturday Night Bash" originally appeared in *River Oak Review*; "The Hill" in *The Union Street Review*; "The Muslim Kite Fighters" in *Clifton Magazine;* "Flying Down to Bombay" in *Other Voices*; "Argos" in *The Long Pond Review*; "Penumbra" in *The Distillery*; "When Hermes Pan Ruled the World" (as "Waiting for the Music") in *Sidewalks*; "Doris" in *E.L.F.*; "The Bus on the Via Triumphans" in *The Panhandler*; "The Game Room" in *Oasis*; and "The Fort" in *Metropolitan*.

For
Brooke and David, Heather and Tom

"Music I heard with you was more than music,
And bread I broke with you was more than bread."

Conrad Aiken

CONTENTS

FOREWORD

TEN DEFINITIONS OF A SHORT STORY

A short story is . . .

1 . . . a novel in a wristwatch, a highly compressed collection of cogs, gears, springs, jewels, and symbols designed to engage the mysteries and processes of time and turn a writer into a precision jeweler who has to make sense of it all.

2 . . . a wild-eyed gypsy woman dancing a bacchanal totally inappropriate for the occasion, with no real beginning or end, just a seductive middle which one watches in a mixture of horror and fascination, wondering about the source of possession in a person who dances like this.

3 . . . the sudden opening and closing of a door leaving one to wonder what was revealed in the quick shaft of light that dazzled one momentarily.

4 . . . a focused narrative between four and forty-five pages long with a beginning, middle, and end, centered around a person who wants something, another who prevents, and a conclusion which is inevitable and yet un-anticipated.

5 . . . an overheard, observed conversation between two people at the table next to yours in the restaurant, briefly uninterrupted by the distraction of the waiter, host, or other guest, allowing you to steal a healthy slice of someone else's life.

6 . . . a cataclysmic eruption of surrealistic action or terror into the ordinary world around you, forcing you to make decisions in a hurry.

7 . . . the looking down a forest path to see if you want to go that way or not.

8 . . . a sudden breeze that plays around your neck and tickles you, suggesting that there's a delightful secret in the universe you may be able to unravel.

9 . . . a nightmare or dream that doesn't make sense and you must write it down for someone wiser than you to interpret.

10 . . . a saved message on your answering machine, a message you are reluctant to erase for some reason.

Roger Lee Kenvin

THE CANTABRIGIAN ROWING SOCIETY'S SATURDAY NIGHT BASH

All right, I admit it, I'm the scuzz what wrote "I hate the poor" on the wall of Trinity's Gate. I'm damn glad I done it, too. It speaks perfectly about my general attitude toward society and all, lookit, if you get the total picture of my True Brit sociological mores and Judeo-Christian ethics, knowing that that kind of crap interests all who read.

And before you try to outsmart me, let me say right here that I hate Margaret Thatcher, too, and her son, the Major, and all their Serious Money bluestockings who walk all over poor honest shits like myself whenever they've a mind to. But I don't like those bleeding-heart homeless people, either, what won't even try to make a decent living through stealing, lying, or conning the middle-class deadheads the way me and my kind do. We're proud of our Good Works, I'd say. And you know who I hate most of all? Surprise, surprise--the New Poor, the Yankee tourists from America-on-the Hudson, who come over here bitching about how everything is so fucking expensive in Merrie Olde these days, not like days of yore when we was just another Coney Island to the Yanks, only with bangers and mash instead of hot dogs.

Do you see those phony photographers with their greedy Nikkons and Minoltas snapping shots of one another around that gushing fountain? Why'nt those frigging Yanks go back where they came from, huh? Don't they know this fountain's a holy shrine to us resident Cantabrigians? This is where Himself took his morning bath at six a.m., standing up stark naked and giving the whole bloody world a first-class hand-shandy when he wanted to show them the old what for. George Noel Gordon, that's what this god's name was. And when they complained, he flipped them the old Bugger-Off-I'm-Lord-Byron routine, which shut them up, those stupid whey-faced academic poufs. A man like that's got to be my idol, lookit, for all the good he done for the cause of straight-forward individuals like me. Naturally, they sacked him, booted him clear to Hell-in-London-and-Europe, but he got his choice revenge, he did, swigging away at both ladies and gentlemen, he never cared which. He knew what was moving and shaking and what was not. Don't believe that shit about His Nibs moping around tombstones on moonlit nights, writing sad stories about the deaths of kings. Never cared for them at all.

Hey, stupid Yanks, you needn't trouble yourselves to search for his effervescent spirit around here anymore, either. You won't find him enshrined in the chapel with simpering Alfred, Lord Tennyson, Sir Francis Bacon-and-Spam, and old Sir Isaac Noodle-Newton, what fondled luscious red apples in his spare time. Why'nt you try the library, though? Might be in for a bit of a surprise. Who do you think is surveying the whole lot of them now in a great big, superior statue somebody put up in his honor as the afterthought of an obviously slow learner? It appears to me as though Himself has had the last laugh after all, and it does my troubled heart good.

I really do hate the New Poor. How can you trust them? Bunch of Yanks pouring through here disguised as tourists, looking for toilets and beef-burger places? Why'nt they go back to Pittsburgh or Chicken-on-the-Car-and-the-Car-Won't-Go? I know all about their lot, sleazing around in their Venice Beach shades and California shorts, with their Cybill Shepherd Reeboks, sucking around this town, looking for some bloke with a pole to take them punting on the Cam, which they won't want to pay for or otherwise complain that it's too dear for their poverty-stricken little American plastic pocketbooks. And who do you suppose they often select to be their very own Royal Imperial British Chauffeur? That's right--Yours Truly, The Poorhouse Kid himself. Not Prince Charlie, not Mark Phillips, just this semi-literate itinerant immigrant from Dublin to Great Harwood in Lancashire to Cambridge-up-the-Arse, England. You might put it that I'm in the Tourist Trade. You could call me Thomas Cook, Jr., if you've a mind to. You could call me Thatcher-Major's bastard son, Master Noblesse Oblige, Jr. of the 1990s.

Hey, Frank Sinatra, I'm talking to you, man. Lookit, I did it, too. Everything I got, I worked hard for. So, scooby-dooby-do-do, to you, folks.

Lookit, I have learned a few useful things in my trade, as they say. One of them's religion, and especially the power of the Almighty. A god has got to be of some value to his followers, don't he? So I find out first what don't these poor note-taking Yanks know about L.B.--which is usually considerable--and then I build on that and wing it from there. I talk familiarly about Bonivard and Childe Harold. I quote from *Don Juan* and remind them it rimes with "true one." I talk about Manfred and the Alps. I invent all kinds of nasties about Augusta Leigh and Annabelle Millbank. I've got serious erotic tales of Countess Teresa Guiccioli and her brothers. That opens up their eyes a bit, you can imagine.

I recommend Newstead Abbey to them and give them directions as to how to get there. "It's Mecca," I say. "You've got to go there before you die." I tell them about the struggle for Greek independence and make up this cock-and-bull story about why Himself was heading for the isles of Greece when he died. I tell them he really died of Aids. Who knows? It could have been.

I link the Greece that L.B. knew with the Middle East situation now. I make every event seem important, give every detail a certain pressing urgency. I drop subtle discriminating comments about Trinity College, as to why it's better than Peterhouse or St. John's. Somewhere along the line it occurs to them that I could be one of Himself's illegitimate great-grandsons. I planted that idea in their noodles at the beginning of my spiel and then I come back to it ever so subtly like a theme in a song of myself, so they get the feeling they have discovered a momentous secret all on their own.

I pull out old portraits of Himself and catch my marks studying me. Of course I've carefully combed my hair to look like his and I deliberately get that same hurt, brooding look into my eyes, so that I let my dark gypsy-like appearance tell it all. I can see the little light bulbs go on in their eyes that say, "What a great story this will make to tell the good neighbors next door when I get back to Yankeeland." It gives me a lift, a positive rush, when I see I'm hooking them. It's better than sex. It's better than the tips they give me when I bring them back to the quay. Punting the New Poor down the banks of the Cam. Nobody punts them the way I do.

This now is what actually happened, if you want to know the whole truth, as Yanks always do. I spotted this shiny blond male ostrich-student from California and his dark Eyetalian-looking mate, loping along, sullying our sacred streets with their bare-legged gaits. I watched as this tall ostrich wafts on down to the quay and talks to John who sends him and his friend over to me. So I say, "Okay, Yanks," put the two of them into my punt, and we're off for a boring hour on this April Saturday just before Easter Sunday. The Jetlag Special, I think to myself, because the two dumb bastards just sit there and stare. They don't ask questions or nothing, just lay back and let me pole them down the Backs, which I do skillfully, and then I bring them on the return to the quay without a single word ever passing from them to me. Lookit, I resented this, as you can readily understand, especially since these dullards didn't even have the decency to tip me or give me so much as a "thank you." It don't amuse me much to have someone I don't really like put me into a corner I don't really want to be in. Such a lack of courtesy. What happened to it crossing the Atlantic from England to the States, I wonder? Did it sink into the briny deep?

If you're with me so far, maybe you'll appreciate well what happened next. I mean, lookit, it was Saturday night. There was a full moon and all, and a few of us were up for it. We'd been at the Anchor and The Free Press, and we were all duded up in our posh blazers and flannels, chatting up the tourist-birds what flew in from Los Angeles and New York, who were hoping to snag an old blue here or there. That's part of it, isn't it? Great Expectations. John and I, and a few others, we figure we've put in time, so let's enjoy a bit of the gravy and trimmings, don't you know? So what's the bother if we swagger a bit and pass ourselves off as undergraduates? What harm does it do? These poor tourist-birds don't know the real students are off on spring hols. We're here. We're available. We're on. That's what counts, I say.

Lookit, we've got a kind of club, you might say—John, Geoff, I, and a few others. We've got these up-market blazers and old school ties, the whole rig, and we've even got a name—The Cantabrigian Rowing Society, which we've also got printed on tee-shirts and all, so we're really casually impressive when we lay it all on some unsuspecting visiting idiot. Sometimes it's good for laughs. Geoff's got this really stupendous Rule-Britannia stuttering accent he puts on. The girls just love it. They always turn to John and me and say, "Geoffrey is so funny and sweet. It must be difficult for him having that mean old penny-pinching lord for a father." I mean, lookit, Geoff's the biggest thief in town. He never had no father. Geoff is light-fingered as all get out. But we always tell the Americans, "Oh, yes, gentle Geoffrey is one lord's son who's certainly got his act together."

Anyway, what you've got is a full moon on this Saturday night. We've downed a few pints and we're heading up Regent Street in the press of people when suddenly what to my wondering eyes should appear but the blond ostrich and the short Eyetalian wearing their little pink shorts and leather thongs and sporting those tantalizing Malibu tans. What do you know? I do fear we are headed for a little collision—the

New Brits versus The Yankee Poor. Could be revenge for a certain earlier little revolution, now, couldn't it?

Blondie and the Eyetalian shift to the right, and then John shifts to the right, which was the wrong way to go. Then the ostrich feints to the left and now is opposite me head on. I can see he don't recognize me, which infuriates me, so I gives him a shove, and he tries to dance by me on the right which is where I moved to also. Lookit, you can't have two bodies in one place, according to Sir Isaac Know-It-All, can you, so I say to him, "Move it, Mate!" and gives him another shove, all the while fingering his passport out of his jacket pocket and hurling it far out over the street, just to show him something, that I am never to be ignored.

John, meanwhile, has shouldered the Eyetalian out of the way, tenderly lifting his wallet while he's at it and passing it to Geoff who picks it off like a football star. But the old ostrich is still standing there like does he need to be sent an engraved invitation as to where to go to next? So I suddenly develop an intense hatred for all the four-eyed ostrichs in the land of California, and I punch this bloke a good one in the left eye, knocking off his glasses, and Geoff whips in to rip off the ostrich's jacket, and then I come in for the kick and send the old ostrich squawking and sprawling right out into the street.

I'm doing my little dance of triumph right on the ostrich's eyeglasses when some other people come up behind us now and stop, frightened, because we look like proper university students and they don't know what the hell's going on. Geoff shouts at them in his best South-of-England accent, "Come on, chaps. Help us clear out these hooligans!" Then he looks at John and me and says, "Let's blow this puke hole!" So off we race as though the whole thing was just your usual Saturday-Night-After-Studying-In-Cambridge-Recreational-Bash.

When we rounded the corner, laughing at our success, we found ourselves at the entrance to Trinity Gate. "Hold on, chaps," I said. "I need to make a personal inscription here." That's when I wrote, "I hate the poor," which I formally christened with my very own golden-lager urine, and I meant it. So let that stand as a warning to all Poor Yanks, especially those with the Age of Innocence in their mugs. I'm likely to wipe it right off their faces. Nobody mucks around with Lord Byron or me. We know what we're about.

Now what do you want to know about "The isles of Greece, the isles of Greece, where burning Sappho loved and sung?" Just ask me!

THE HILL

What I really remember most about that particular day in May, 1939, was the long, slippery climb up the hill. It seemed to me that it was a very threatening day with great pockets of moisture and the smell of lilacs in bloom that one went through along the way. I remember how hard it was to pump that bicycle uphill, although I had ridden it to her house many times before.

I have talked with many other people since about that English spring. Some remember the tremendous thunderstorm we had that night, cracking open the sky over London like some horrible Götterdämmerung. One friend of mine, a poet, told me that William Butler Yeats wrote "The Second Coming" in that year, about a rough beast slouching toward Bethlehem to be born. My friend thought it meant Adolph Hitler. Maybe he was right. It certainly was an odd day for me, I can tell you that.

All along Finchley Road, the chestnut trees were so heavy with humidity that I had to dodge branches of those white flambeaux swatting down at me. I arrived at Maresfield Gardens at the top, and then rode on the sidewalk until I reached the brick house where I leaned my bicycle up against the entrance and patted Lün, the chow, on the head. He would always come around the front to greet visitors. I think he took his guard dog duties very seriously.

Paula met me at the entrance and said Madam was running late, so did I mind waiting a few minutes? I said "No" and checked my pocket to see if the map I had made for Madam was still there. It showed the easiest escape route from Eton. I meant to tell her all about my plan that day.

"Why don't you have a seat here?" asked Paula, pointing to one of those dark, upholstered chairs that seem to want to devour you.

"I'll just wait," I said, meaning I would stand.

"Perhaps you'd like to wait in the garden then," she said, indicating the back of the house where I knew there was a deep, secret garden I had never been to or seen before.

"That will do," I said. "Is that where Lün stays?"

"Yes," said Paula. "Give him a call. He'll show you around." I followed her through the dining room with its Tyrolese painted furniture and out into the garden which was bursting with lilac blooms and contrasting cubes of light and darkness because of the strange sun that day.

"Lün?" I called, and he came bounding around the corner, followed by an old man I first thought was the gardener, but then realized must be Madam's father who I knew lived in the house with her and her mother.

"Hello, boy,"said the old man. "What are you doing out here in the garden?"

"Paula sent me here," I explained. "I am waiting for my appointment." I indicated the third storey where Madam's office was.

"Oh," he said, softening a bit, I thought. "Fearful day, isn't it?"

"Dramatic," I replied.

"It's spring yearning to be summer," the old man said, bending down and delicately spreading green leaves to reveal something near the ground. "Look here. What do you see?"

"They appear to be small strawberries," I said.

"The French call them *frais de bois*. Summer," he said, "It's on the way." He looked up at the sky. It was beginning to spit a bit now. "Once Nature gets these anxious cataclysms out of its system . . . well, we can't stay here and get soaked, can we? Come this way." He led me down a little path until we came to glass doors that went into his study at the back of the house. It was so dark when I entered that I couldn't see anything at first.

"Let me just turn on some lamps."

The old man watched my reactions. I saw his desk, very solid, noticed many objects on it, little statues, sculptures, a whole world of little people in a quiet procession. Books in cases along the wall. A long couch covered with a Turkish rug, a large Persian carpet on the floor. Quite splendid, I thought.

"Sit down," he said, indicating the couch. I sat. He plopped into the green tub chair directly to my right, so that I had to turn to look at him directly. He noticed that this embarrassed me and rose, went and sat at his desk in a weird chair designed so that it looked like the skeleton of a body embracing him. Creepy, I thought.

"I'll tell you a story about strawberries," he said, "but you must not tell Madam I told you." He emphasized the word "Madam" which I think he thought amusing.

"All right," I said. "What is it?"

"When she was a little girl, I took her walking in the fields at Ausse. We came upon wild strawberries, and, she, only about two years old, ate them savagely. Well, naturally, she came down with a violent stomach ache. We thought it best that she not put anything else in her stomach the next day, to give it a rest, you see, but that night, when her mother and I looked in at her, there she slept, but she cried out a whole menu to us. We heard her say clearly, "stwabewwies, wild stwabewwies, omblet, pudden." He laughed. "Do you see? *Traümerei. Die Traümdeutung.* I wrote a whole book about that incident."

I didn't think it was so funny. I couldn't picture Madam as a young child. "Why do you have all these little objects on your desk?" I asked him, thinking him very odd indeed, especially since I noticed he had picked up a hot water bottle and was holding it against the dark blotch on his cheek.

He caught me staring. "I have an ulceration here," he explained. He looked around the room, letting his left hand sweep gently over the many objects on his desk. "Well, these are only objects from other people's tombs, of archaological interest mostly. Which is the one that attracts you most?"

I looked around the room. Some masks looked Greek, like the ones in the British Museum. Others, I could see, were Egyptian, Roman, or Oriental. On his desk there were many smaller objects. One was a small figure riding on an elephant. "That one," I said, pointing to it.

That seemed to please him. "This one?" he asked, holding it up. "Why did you select this one?"

"I like elephants," I told him. "I would like to ride on one like that little person."

"That little person is Hannibal," said the old man. "Do you know who he was?"

"Yes," I said. "He crossed the Alps."

"He was a Carthaginian," said the man. "That's why I admired him. He dared to take on a whole Roman empire in the Second Punic War. He put elephants into his cavalry, was the commander in Spain, and in 216 B.C. at Canae won one of the most brilliant military victories ever. I think he was a man of great courage and daring. I admire those qualities very much."

Suddenly, the door from the hallway was opened and Paula looked in. "Here he is," she called to someone just behind her. Madam rushed into the room.

"Viktor," she said to me. "Here you are. I am so sorry to be late. My other appointment just ran overtime."

"Mine never showed up," said the old man. "Viktor and I have been talking about Hannibal. I think we are in agreement about him."

"Well, Viktor," Madam said. "Shall we go up to my office now?"

"Might as well stay right here," said her father. "Come in and join us. Is it still sprinkling out there?" He looked toward the garden.

"It may storm," said Madam.

"Well, then, we'll just stay put. Don't argue with Nature," said her father. "Don't you agree, Viktor?"

"Yes, sir," I said.

Madam intervened, as though she had to explain me to her father. "We were just talking last time about the intentions of Viktor's parents . . ."

"What are their intentions?" asked the old man, rising from his desk now and looking out into the darkening garden.

"They want to send me to Eton," I answered.

"Very good," said the old man. "That should be a delightful prospect."

"No," I said. "It isn't."

"Viktor wishes to go back to Graz, Father," said Madam in a careful voice.

The old man came over and looked me close in the face. He still held up the hot water bottle to his cheek. I thought his ulcer gave off a very bad smell. "That isn't possible, is it, son?"

"Yes, it is."

"But Austria has been absorbed by the Nazis now."

"The family is Jewish," said Madam.

"We are Jewish also," the old man said. "Hannibal, too, was a semite. But you, Viktor, you have no armies and no elephants, do you?"

"I don't like England," I said. "I will not go to Eton. I have planned my escape. Here's my map." I pulled out the elaborate map I had drawn. He took it. He and Madam both looked at it. I watched to see if they would laugh at me, but they didn't. They took me at my word, I could see.

"How old are you?" asked her father.

"Fourteen."

The man spread out my map on his desk, smoothing out the wrinkles in the paper with his hand. He looked at his daughter as though calculating something. "We must plan this escape carefully," he said. "Now then," he said to me. "Come, show us exactly how you plan to do this."

I showed them where I had marked the X in the hall where I would be staying and where the door was that I would pass through, and how I would get past the warden and the main gate and then into the town and out on the road to Windsor from which I would catch a coach back to London.

"Very ingenious," said the old man. "I think it will work very well. This part makes sense. But you must reconsider the part about returning to Graz just now."

"It's where I belong," I said.

"Vienna is where I belong," he shouted abruptly. "Do you think I wanted to come here to London?"

"Father," said his daughter, "perhaps Viktor and I should go up to my study. . ."

"No," said the old man. "We'll have it out here. I lived at Bergasse 19 for forty-seven years," he said to me, his voice trembling with strong emotion. "Then the Nazis came in and defiled my home with a swastika. They burned my books. They dissolved my organization. We were forced into exile here. Four of my sisters are left behind there. I don't know what will become of them. They are arresting Jews. Is this what you want for yourself now?"

"I can survive," I said.

"Nobody can survive," he said, "until this madman is silenced."

"We have been talking about all aspects of this situation," said Madam. "His father is in Austria. His mother sent him to me."

"My father is in danger,"I said. "I have to find him. I want to help him. Is that so strange? Why does my mother want to put me away in a place like Eton in a time like this?"

"Do you have his father's name?" the old man asked his daughter.

"Yes."

"We can try to locate him. We have friends . . ."

"His mother has tried to make inquiries," Madam explained.

"Viktor," said the old man, "you will also have our assistance. We shall talk some more. When do you see him next?" he asked his daughter.

"In a fortnight," she said. "Isn't that your next appointment?"

"I think so," I said. "If I come." I felt at that moment like rushing out of the room. Why had she violated my confidence and revealed me to her father as a foolish boy who could never do the right thing, but instead always went against his mother's wishes?

"Let me write to some friends," said the old man. "I will talk with you when I hear." He cuffed me on the head in a friendly way with his left hand.

Paula knocked at the door and opened it. "The afternoon post has arrived," she said. "It has stopped raining."

"I'd better go now," I said, looking out toward the garden. "Before it storms. My bicycle's out front."

The old man put out his hand. I shook it. "We'll help," he said. His eyes were bright as he said it. I remember thinking, "He will."

"Thank you," I replied.

"Remember," he said, "Hannibal put a lot of thought into his plans, too."

"Yes, sir," I said, going out and getting my bicycle.

I rode home, feeling more secure. The light intensified the colors along the way. It was as though I were caught in a giant terrarium of plane trees, chestnuts, maples, rhododendrons, roses, and lilacs, a little specimen of a human being in a great greenhouse of a universe. It wasn't until after I got home that the real thunderstorm broke. I remember my mother being very frightened by it, and I can still hear the firebell clanging and see the firewagon that raced down our street on its way to rescue someone in trouble.

Each time I made the journey back to Maresfield Gardens, the best thing about it was that I had the feeling I was leaving the grey city behind and entering into the hidden garden where the old man was God and Madam was his mother, even though I knew she really was his daughter. I always thought this, but I never told anyone about my feelings, even them.

Through the summer months, I saw only Madam for my appointments. She would say, "My father says 'No news yet,'" and I did not see him again until very early in September when she said he wanted to talk with me. She led me into his study. He was sitting on his couch, looking much the same, perhaps a little more tired. He held out his hand, but did not get up and walk around this time.

"Viktor," he said. "Why don't you sit at my desk?" Madam pulled out the chair for me.

"No thanks," I said. "I'll just stand." Madam put the chair back at the desk again.,

"I have had some word from friends in Graz. This comes to us from Bregenz across Lake Constance. It appears that your father has been arrested by the Nazis and is not now in Graz. This is all that we have heard."

"No," I screamed at him. "It is not true."

The old man reached out both his arms to me, but I pulled back. "My sisters, too, have not been heard from. We must all put our heads together now and plan what is to be done. You can do nothing alone."

"We'll go up now to my study," said Madam to her father, practically shoving me out the door. I was angry, confused, crying. I didn't hate the old man, just the rotten news he brought, throwing it down to me as though I were his Job.

That was the last time I saw him. I remember that my next appointment in September was canceled abruptly. My mother called me into our sitting room and told me some sad news. She said that the old man had died. She said Madam had sent a message to me in the form of a medallion that had belonged to her father. It showed a strong Hannibal on one side and the Alps on the other.

A lucky medal for me in 1939. After Poland fell in that year, England got into the war. Lithuania and Czechoslovakia were swept away also. I went off to Eton to please my mother, and I stopped going to see Madam because there was no need to escape anymore. Norway, France, the Netherlands, and Belgium were conquered.

Somehow, my mother and I managed to survive the terrible blitz that began in September 1940. I went into the British Army in 1943, and on V-E Day in 1945, I learned that my father was never coming back. He had died in Büchenwald. That was the saddest day of my life, but the happiest for everybody else. Later, I heard that three of the old man's sisters had also perished in the camp at Auschwitz.

In 1948, my mother became seriously ill. She wanted to return to Graz. It was not an easy thing to do. The first thing we did when we got there was to plan a new garden in the back yard. We still believed in possibilities.

THE MUSLIM KITE FIGHTERS

Lepers shoot out their stunted tentacles toward us and glassy-eyed monkeys leer as we drive by on the bridge. Crouched on their haunches, with hands flopping out in front, the monkeys watch for just one opening. Why don't they leave us alone? The bridge is such a narrow passage. They know they've got us where they want us.

"*Chelly-ow*," says Mahmood Hassim, flailing out a leg at a monkey that threatens to make a pass at us. This monkey clutches an incongruous red kite in his hand that he has stolen from someone, probably a woman or a girl, who passed too close to him. He jeers at us and holds out the kite toward us, taunting us with his thieving superiority. These monkeys are not to be trusted. One flew down from a tamarind tree a week ago and bit a chunk the size of an apple out of a woman's arm. She was eating bread. The monkey wanted that bread and got it.

We are heading for Bundurbagh Circus today. We will meet Rahat there. Rahat is my cook and chief servant. I am his Social Security and Blue Cross. I am buying him eyeglasses today. He is at the oculist's now, having his eyes fitted for glasses. He is forty years old. It has just been discovered that he needs glasses.

Arshad is riding with me in the rickshaw. He is a university student, about twenty-two years old, slight of build. I am one of the persons he collects. He specializes in English and Americans. He came up to me one day when I first arrived and said, "May I help you? You look as though you are lost. I know everything. I can take you everywhere." I am suspicious of this know-it-all, but I accept him as my guide because he is right; I need him to help me through this maze.

Mahmood Hassim pedals the rickshaw, a three-wheeled contraption that I bought for him. He has driven for me almost every day since I have been here. I paid $150 for the rickshaw so that it would give him economic independence.

He is eighteen and was married when he was thirteen. He wears a brown wool shirt and pants that I gave him from my own wardrobe. I can take just so much of the searing poverty I find in Chand Bagh.

I am in India as a consulting engineer for my firm which is bringing the first extensive air-conditioning to the governmental buildings in Chand Bagh. It has taken months of negotiations, often very delicate, intensely personal ones, to get anything accomplished. The bureacracy is staggering.

I have a three-room apartment in the home of Justinian and Opal Sharaf, wealthy Indian Christians, who live on Faizabad Road. Their house sits in a giant rose garden and is surrounded by high walls bordered by poinsettia hedges. There are bars on all our windows, designed to keep out monkeys and thieves. We have seven servants in all and three dachshunds who are trained to watch for cobras that might slither into our compound at night from the nearby mango trees. The Sharafs have a small automobile which they bring out on rare occasions. There aren't many cars in Chand Bagh. We are located in Uttar Pradesh, the largest province in northern India.

It is a clear day with a water color-blue sky overhead. It is very early, a little after 7:30 a.m. now. We have gotten an early start because today is a special festival day when everybody will fly kites, thousands of them, dancing in the sky over Chand Bagh. Arshad says he does not really know how or why this kite-flying craze got started. He thinks it goes back to the time of the Moguls. He remembers that he heard that Wajid Ali Shah used to fly kites as well as act and dance in the celebrations he wrote for his many wives and himself. That was in the first part of the nineteenth century, Arshad tells me. He recites a few lines from a poem that Wajid Ali Shah wrote for his most beloved wife. Arshad looks me straight in the eye as he recites it with passion. It embarrasses me a little the way he looks into me and almost blames me for something, I don't know what. Arshad has a prodigious memory for everything he reads.

Could a February day ever be as clear as this one? Even the most appalling poverty looks beautiful to the eye when washed with this strong sunlight. This is the best time of the year in northern India. It makes me feel good, active, responsive to the pulse of life around me. I feel quite Indian, although I know I am merely a white American who is startled by his own unhandsome reflection in mirrors. I wish I had a more attractive brown skin like those of the people I see around me.

Arshad, the collector of English and Americans, is disturbed by my fastidious avoidance of them, but I am curious about Indians and want always to be with them. I study Hindi four nights a week with a young woman from the university who comes to my place. Arshad said why didn't I ask him, he knows Urdu as well as Hindi. I told him I needed a simplified approach, that Meena, my tutor, was highly recommended, and that I was learning quite well. Arshad listened patiently, but was obviously annoyed. Maybe because Meena is a Hindu. Arshad, Rahat, and Mahmood Hassim are all Muslims.

"Kee-yun op runjeedah henh?" I ask Mahmood Hassim, wondering why he is not singing a song as he usually does. *"Nuheen ganna adj?"*

Arshad translates Mahmood Hassim's reply: "He says that he is sad because he does not know why."

"Beemer?"

"No, not sick," comes back the reply.

I think Mahmood Hassim will be lucky if he lives to be twenty-five. His brother died of tuberculosis. Other rickshaw-wallahs burn themselves out with drugs or drink. Some live only for gambling. Some have been found dead of exposure in their rickshaws on extremely cold nights.

We ride along in silence, past masons swarming all over the new lingam temple being erected to Shiva. Now we whip through the ruined gates of the Victoria Palace, out the other side, into a long street, damp and musty, and then a great thrust out into the traffic of Bundurbagh Circus, a merry-go-round of rickshaws, bicycles, and pedestrians with the Ashoka Pillar in the center, crowned by crouching lions, and all around the Circus arcaded shops of yellow and white sandstone.

We aim for a shop with a large sign that reads:

MUSHTAQ
GRANDSON OF MOHAMMED ISHAW
AND MOHAMMED IBRAHIM
MANUFACTURING OPTICIANS

Rahat waves us in for a landing. We are to help him decide which frames are right for his face. The optician offers us a tray of frames. Four possibilities: red plastic ones costing 6 rupees, brown plastic ones at 18 rupees, ones with thin gold stripes for 22 rupees, and a last set of frames heavy with gold at 35 rupees. The brown plastic ones look best on Rahat, in my opinion, but it is obvious that he favors the thick gold ones. He keeps fingering them.

"Rahat," I say, indicating the heavy gold frames in his hand. "I think those are the frames you really should have. Consider them."

Rahat considers them, turning them over carefully.

Arshad, however, holds up the cheap red ones. "These are the best," he says with a nervous little laugh,"and the least expensive." He shoots out a side glance at me.

"No," I say, vetoing the suggestion. "I like the ones in your hand, Rahat."

Rahat tries them on again, takes a long look at himself in the mirror, looks back at the doorway to where Mahmood Hassim is standing quietly taking in the whole scene. Now, as I study Rahat, I feel that the substantial frames seem just right for his chiseled features, his tall bearing. Then Rahat turns back to the oculist and holds out the frames to him. "These" he says. Arshad makes a low whistling noise of disapproval. There is something going on between Rahat and Arshad. I am worried that my favor, my approbation, is at the heart of it.

The glasses will be ready on Friday. We agree to come back then. Arshad and I climb back into the rickshaw. Rahat has his bicycle which he will ride. "Friday at three," he says happily to the oculist. He is off to the bazaar now for shopping. He will buy kites and string for us. The kites will soar today, he promises me, his brown eyes opening wide to show the limitless possibilities this recreation will afford. He will also buy tonight's dinner, perhaps prepare a biriani covered with silver paper. There will also be papaya for dessert tonight, he promises.

"This is your servant, Rahat," Justinian Sharaf had said when he first presented Rahat to me eight months ago. I thought this a very peremptory, colonial way to introduce someone. I shook Rahat's hand warmly to show my displeasure with Justinian's stuffy Anglo-Indian formality. But I soon learned that Rahat, like Justinian, longed for the pre-1947 days of British dominion. "In English-time," Rahat would say to me often, "We would have sixty, maybe seventy people in for dinner. First would come sherry, then soup, then fish--seven courses. We would have wine. You will be inviting people, sahib?" he would add hopefully. His face would always cloud over in disappointment when I told him I could only entertain two or three people at the most, and over a simple meal, nothing grand or imperial, in the style he remembered.

But Rahat is a superb professional, taking pride and care in every meal he prepares and being responsive to my every need. His very name means "Pleasure" in his language. His kingdom is the kitchen, a separate building at the end of the rose garden. He somehow concocts American hamburgers, buckwheat cakes with syrup, omelets, and fried chicken, out of the ingredients he studiously purchases at the market every day. I never go to market with him. I never set foot in his kitchen. Rahat is an artist, a magician, and a kind, considerate man. But to him I am always "Sahib," the one on

whom he is dependent. His salary has doubled since I have
been here. "Whatever you say, Sahib," he says. "Whatever
you do."

To Arshad, I am perhaps the prize star in his collection.
Arshad has never been farther from Chand Bagh than to the
library in Lucknow, and his current friends include English
oddities like Dr. Dry, an Anglican clergyman, and Mr. Piggott,
a geologist who sputters and stutters so much in an upper-
class style that you can't understand him anyway.

Arshad is more difficult to figure out than Rahat. Arshad is
educated, intellectual. He has a good command of English.
Does he resent being Indian now that he knows so much? He
makes references to Oxford, Cambridge, and Harvard. He is
curious about them. He wants to know everything I think
about them. He shows me every poem he writes. His poems
are all love poems addressed to some ill-defined person,
maybe to the idea of a person. He tells me his father has two
wives. Arshad expects that he himself will be married one
day. He laughs when I ask if he will have two wives also. He
says he doesn't think he will be able to afford them. His
grandfather has four wives, he confides. We both laugh,
thinking of Arshad's spindly-legged grandfather with his own
personal harem.

To Mahmood Hassim, I must seem like some kind of
apostle sent down by Allah to heap benefits upon him.
Mahmood Hassim has a well-developed sense of kismet.
When I gave him his rickshaw, he thanked Allah, not me. He
is an innocent who will not survive the spring of his Indian
youth, I'm afraid. He dreams of Calcutta. I have this fear that
when I leave India, he will sell his rickshaw, move to Calcutta
and be swallowed up forever in that teeming anthill.

Three among millions—an intellectual, a professional, and
a subservient. That all three are Muslims is the luck of the
town. Chand Bagh is half Muslim and half Hindu. My Hindu
neighbor, Mr. Barghava, is a high-caste Brahmin. He invited
me to dinner, saying that in the old days he couldn't have
done so because it was thought that all pale-faced people

were suffering from leprosy. This pointed up my status as an outsider in India. Mr. Barghava is not my favorite person. My three Muslim friends do not condescend. They seek my friendship. For once in my life I am the prize.

Now it is afternoon. We have moved up toward the blue-domed heaven overhead. We are standing on the roof of the Sharafs' house. The sky is crowded with kites. Hundreds of people are out flying kites of all sizes and colors. Rahat takes charge now, picking up a brightly-colored spool of string and a black-and-silver kite. He offers to show me how to fly a kite. I am to select one from the several he has brought with him. I choose a bright red one with a long tail. Rahat takes it from me to demonstrate his technique. I laugh at the thought of a kite-flying lesson at my age, but I am amazed at the ease with which Rahat handles the kite and sends it soaring into the sky.

Soon Arshad appears with a gold kite in his hand and joins us on the rooftop. Rahat, however, is a master of dynamics, maneuvering my red kite this way and that way. He manipulates, pulls, reels in the string adroitly, like an expert puppeteer. Arshad watches him closely like a predatory cat. Suddenly, Arshad launches his gold kite into the air. It dances provocatively near Rahat's. A deep frown fills Rahat's face now. He reels in his kite, bites off the string with his teeth, and replaces the string with another, shinier string that looks like fish line.

"What are you doing?" I ask.

"Glass string for cutting," Rahat says tersely, sending the red kite up into the billowy atmosphere again.

Arshad grins confidently. "We shall see," he says.

What is going on, I wonder? Some sort of game? A contest? There is an unpleasant grim humor now in the stance and attitudes of my friends. Something there is flying in the sky that is more than just a kite. I see now that Rahat's kite is attacking Arshad's with quick, deft moves. Rahat is attempting to cut the string of Arshad's kite just below its tail.

It bothers me that the red kite was supposed to be my kite. Rahat was supposed to be giving me a lesson.

Arshad starts reining in his kite now, bringing it down in a long arcing swoop. Rahat's kite follows it. I am astonished at the skill and the ruthlessness of the two men. Suddenly, Rahat's kite flies into Arshad's kite like a killer cock in a cockfight. Now Arshad's kite is floating limply away, off toward a cloud, higher now, growing smaller, disappearing, gone. Arshad looks disappointed. He avoids looking at me. Instead, he tells me he will see me in a few days. Then he vanishes.

I am angry with Arshad and this abrupt end to what should have been a pleasant event. I turn to test Rahat's reaction. He is elated. He looks me straight in the eyes and smiles. Something important has been determined, I know.

THE SHAKESPEARE PROBLEM

In an effort to be open and democratic, Mary Moses Deuteronomy decided that tea would be taken out in the open under the clear blue Indian sky. Imtiaz obligingly arranged the table with three chairs, and Mary Moses motioned to English teachers Dr. Alison Thrace and Miss Immaculata Conception to follow her.

"It is this overruling of our committee's decision which is most disturbing," she said, looking around to see if the others disagreed.

The golden-haired Alison lowered her gaze into her cup and sipped her tea in a deliberately quiet manner which didn't escape Mary Moses' notice. Immaculata, thin, timid, glanced at Alison expectantly, as though she might say something. Alison expressed slight annoyance toward the shy Indian teacher and spoke directly to Mary Moses: "But, Dr. Deuteronomy, it is a Shakespearean play that he is directing. Surely, you find that commendable?"

"Shakespeare is always commendable," snapped out Mary Moses in her deepest, most correct elocutionary voice. "It is not the quality of the substitution that is reprehensible; it is that there has been any substitution at all."

"But he is our guest director . . ." began Alison.

Mary Moses set down her tea cup noisily. "That is precisely the point," she said. "As a guest director, Dr. Connor should have abided by the committee's original decision."

"Well, I really think . . ." Alison tried again, hesitating now because she felt her temper rising.

"The students did love *Twelfth Night* last year," Immaculata said warmly.

Mary Moses fixed her with her eye: "That was different. Dr. Thrace directed that. It was not the circus that *As You Like It* has become."

Alison finished her tea slowly, pointedly setting her tea cup in the saucer quietly. Imtiaz whisked it away, as though anxious to end the ceremony which, he could see, had an unwanted undercurrent of acrimony. Alison casually smoothed out her sari and adjusted the pin on her shoulder. "Well, you are being unreasonable about the whole thing," she said.

A swift intake of air on Mary Moses' part. How impertinent this golden Anglo-Saxon goddess from Oxford was. "Dr. Connor is the one being unreasonable," she replied. "The students are interested in him, not Shakespeare. You must be blind, Alison," she added.

"I think you are overreacting," said Alison, standing up now, anxious to terminate this obtuse conversation. "You forget that your choice of *A Majority of One* was not really a terribly popular one, even with the committee."

"It was a much wiser choice," Mary Moses countered. "It is a moral play. A Jewish woman from Brooklyn and a Japanese man meeting on an ocean liner. Surely, the parable is clear."

"Dear Dr. Deuteronomy," said Immaculata gently. "You must admit that Shakespeare offers parables and parallels as well."

Mary Moses fixed Immaculata with her evil eye now, daring her to avert her gaze. "You seem to forget, Miss Conception, that my doctorate is in Shakespeare. I am surely a better judge of moral values in his work than you are. Your field is Victorian poetry."

"I only meant that certainly there must be moral values in *As You Like It*, if only we will search for them," Immaculata replied in a voice that trailed off.

"I'm late for my appointment," said Alison, glancing at her wrist watch. "You must excuse me."

"Very well. We shall adjourn. I gather I have been unreasonable," Mary Moses said using her *mea culpa* voice.

"Oh, no, not at all," said Immaculata.

"The students are enjoying the rehearsals," said Alison. "Why don't you just wait and see how the whole production turns out?"

"Apparently, that is what must be done," said Mary Moses, waving both Alison and the traitorous Immaculata out of her presence. Imtiaz opened the door to the building for them, giving each a slight bow. "Shall I be getting you some aspirin?" he asked Mary Moses when her two guests had gone.

"Yes, thank you. That would be very nice," said Mary Moses, settling back now on her caneback settee, having been bested once again by that serene Alison, so rational and glib with her opinions, making Mary Moses appear so humorless and reactionary in even the slightest of contexts, as though Mary Moses were some kind of obdurate Marxist, just the flint-edged image she always fought so hard to resist.

Image: Mary Moses had no mirrors in her office, nor in her bedroom. She didn't trust them, didn't want them, since she couldn't bear what she saw in the looking-glass, only the way she sounded, that wonderful alto voice speaking English correctly, precisely, with the right kind of educated inflection so widely respected in the English-speaking world. But the mirror always revealed to her what she was and always would be: An unattractive, small woman of both Indian and African parentage, dressed in an expensive silk sari, reflecting an aristocratic background that pointed up the disparity between her own truthful origin and the shining, artificial world of her educational aspirations which made her feel guilty and question motivation, purpose, and goal in herself and others. Still, she had that glorious diction and sonorous voice, and she couldn't, wouldn't give them up. Language was her passion.

Mary Moses had been born in Maharashtra to an Indian woman of Dravidian ancestry and an African father who soon abandoned his wife and five children. Mary Moses' only memories of her father were how afraid she was of him with his drinking and smoking and his striking out at her mother and all the children. She remembered the trembling in the night, the snuggling close to the nearest warm body in bed, the dampness in their small village hut.

As a child, she had been perilously fragile. She pictured herself as an undernourished big-eyed child with a giant brain, almost prescient. She absorbed her mother's strong will and stoicism. She listened to the teachers in the village and to anyone who seemed to talk sense. She learned to use the few simple things around her to best advantage, all for one purpose, to hold the family together, because she could see that is what her mother wanted and that is what her father betrayed.

She remembered the time she was sixteen and the school authorities from Bombay arrived for a visit. They came through, causing a great noise and raising of dust in their jeeps, and held secret, distant conferences with the village leaders and teachers. Suddenly, Mary Moses found herself segregated from her school friends, selected, she could tell, for some signal honor that meant she would have to leave her mother, brothers, and sisters. The thought frightened her. The visitors all jabbered in English among themselves, but she could catch bits of their conversation when they spoke in Hindi to the village authorities. Nobody consulted her or her mother, but finally one of the teachers took her mother aside and spoke something into her ear that pleased her mother and caused her to smile the smile that Mary Moses interpreted as the smile of greatest pleasure--one rarely seen on her mother's face and only on the happiest occasions.

"And so it came to pass that I was taken up by the educationists and began life as a full scholarship student at Chand Bagh College," is the way Mary Moses later liked to refer to this period in her life. "It was quite like a Dickens' novel. I became a person of great expectations." At Chand Bagh, in that great place of light and learning for women, the major transformation of her life began. She no longer was a *harijan*, but became converted to Christianity since Chand Bagh had been founded by an American Methodist missionary, and she took on her new name, Mary Moses Deuteronomy. "Mary" for tenderness and mercy, qualities represented by her mother and teachers. "Moses" because she realized that she was really a tough Old Testament person who abided by a few inviolable principles. And "Deuteronomy" because she had first read that book in the King James version of the *Bible* and was instantly struck by the beauty and appropriateness of its literary style.

She was a student at Chand Bagh from her sixteenth to her twenty-first year. Upon graduation, she was invited to stay on as a part-time lecturer in English. But, just as she began her teaching, her mother became critically ill at home, and Mary Moses had to leave to nurse her mother through her final illness and to run her mother's household. She later counted it among her greatest accomplishments that she had been able to convert her mother, one brother, and two of her sisters to Christianity during this time. When she returned to Chand Bagh after her mother's death, the administration rewarded her by sending her off to England to study for a six months' period.

If Chand Bagh had been a revelation to Mary Moses, England was even more so. Here was a whole country, predominantly Christian, remarkably clean, with whizzing cars, high-rise buildings, amazing shops, and pastoral parks. In London, she read, talked with people from all over the world, visited the British Museum, and listened. She took holidays on the Isle of Skye and in Warwickshire. She traced Wordsworth's and Coleridge's steps in Cumberland. And she found time, wherever she was, to seek out Salvation Army shelters, to help people with problems, especially fellow Indians, alcoholics, and women who had been abused. Every night, the good Mary Moses thanked God in her prayers for making her an agent between India and England. She knew that she could never give up her goal of service to people who needed her.

But England forced Mary Moses to see herself the way many others saw her. She would sometimes forget who she was, until, suddenly, she would catch a glimpse of herself in a department store window or mirror and see that she wasn't one of those Anglo-Saxon beauties who fascinated her. However, she saw in her reflection strength and purpose and she thanked her God who had gifted her with these. All her life, Mary Moses could not help sliding toward sainthood.

When she returned to India, Mary Moses now came into her prime. She recreated Dickens' London for her students. She chatted familiarly about John Keats, Jane Austen, and the Brontes. She had personally re-traced Boswell's and Johnson's journey to the Hebrides. She knew exactly where Newstead Abbey was and where Harriet Shelley drowned herself in the Serpentine. Her students found her intriguing, her speaking voice mesmerizing, and her judgments amusing. As one of them put it, "Dr. Deuteronomy is like a country road in some remote part of India that one must walk down, not ride down, because there is no other way to go, so you must just make up your mind to enjoy it, and it really is rather beautiful." Her students who were Hindus, Muslims, and Christians all felt she taught them well. They took to heart her central precept that knowing and doing what was best for others was what Christianity was all about.

After Chand Bagh set up an international exchange program with the United States, Mary Moses, naturally, was chosen as the first representative from India. She was assigned to a small college in South Carolina that was predominantly rural and black, but those problems were easy ones for her. The real difficulty was that she could not get Shakespeare across to students whose soft, Southern accents she couldn't readily understand. Why didn't they enunciate? They, in turn, thought she was a harmless eccentric, a little pretentious, from a disease-and-disaster-ridden country none of them ever wanted to visit and a promoter of a culture from England that seemed alien to everything they knew.

In fact, Mary Moses' arrival in the United States had been a jarring experience. She had been hurtled from Kennedy airport via a speeding taxi into the Jumping Jack flash of New York City, glowing like a gaudy pinball machine in a hellish universe. People talked in rapid grunts or outlandish superlatives. Nothing made sense. The I.R.T. subway ride was horrifying. Fifth Avenue with its shops and St. Patrick's Cathedral were disappointing compared to London. She looked in vain for order, logic, and private space, but found none in New York.

Still, Mary Moses made the effort to have new experiences, to keep an open, positive outlook. When she went back to Chand Bagh she brought with her new authors—Imamu Amiri Baraka, Maya Angelou, Toni Morrison, Alice Walker, in addition to poets like Sylvia Plath and Adrienne Rich, and novelists like Faulkner, Steinbeck, Updike, and Mailer. Unfortunately, her Indian students only showed a passing interest in any of them. They wanted news of Disneyland, Bon Jovi, Madonna, and Elvis Presley. Mary Moses could only chalk it up to youthful stupidity and try to steer the conversation back to Shakespeare and values once again. The good playwright could be so satisfactory when you wanted him to be. Mary Moses was proud of her great discovery, upon which she had based her doctoral thesis, that Shakespeare's tragedies all turn pretty much on Mosaic law—*King Lear* on "Thou shalt honor thy father and mother," *Hamlet* on "Thou shalt not kill" and "Thou shalt not commit adultery," *Macbeth* on "Thou shalt not covet thy neighbor's possessions," and so on.

Now, at age fifty, Mary Moses Deuteronomy was disturbed by the unwelcome presence of Dr. Harrison Connor, who had arrived from Yale with a doctorate in theatre history and a lot of directing experience. Since he was to be their guest director for only one year, he said he

wouldn't follow the drama committee's suggestion to direct
A Majority of One, but, instead, would do Shakespeare's *As
You Like It*, reversing the original all-male convention by
replacing it with an all-female one. He argued that the
transvestism in the central character of Rosalind was more
easily suited to the all-female environment of Chand Bagh
College.

Mary Moses did not like Harrison Connor's cavalier
attitude. She did not approve of his use of the word
"transvestism" at all. It was inflammatory, suggestive. It
indicated he knew too much about the hidden springs of
sexuality in individuals, dangerous areas by her standards. She
was afraid, also, that Shakespeare might let her down
personally, or that he might be exposed for what he really
was, or both. Mary Moses, in her doctoral thesis, had carefully
glossed over the many frivolous comedies Shakespeare had
written. In short, she disliked *As You Like It*, but she could
not publicly say so because that would not only show a lack
of taste, it might also spell her ruin as the leading
Shakespearean authority at Chand Bagh, and it would most
certainly disprove the central point of her thesis.

She felt irritable after hearing students discussing *As You
Like It* in the halls. Where else but from Harrison Connor
were the students getting the notion that "Audrey" and
"bawdy" were related? That "country" in the Phoebe-Silvius
scenes had an inappropriate meaning? That Celia's and
Oliver's problems were sexual frustration? That the Rosalind-
Orlando scenes involved suppressed homosexuality? What
was this director telling these young women? Mary Moses
considered the bizarre implications in the ending of this light
comedy: The whole thing is capped off by the Roman god of
marriage, Hymen, arriving and pairing off all the couples in a
dance-off of ecstatic connubial bliss. No doubt about it, *As
You Like It* was wantonly licentious. How could anyone make
anything moral out of it, unlike Alison Thrace's version of
Twelfth Night last year where the opening line, "If music be
the food of love, play on," became the central motif in the

production and was reinforced by twanging sitars and sarods carrying out the pretty music notion of the play?

Imtiaz returned now with the aspirin. "Thank you, Imtiaz," she said, taking three aspirin. "I'll just take these with another cup of tea. I think I'll sit here a little longer. I must think through this Shakespeare problem."

"Yes, memsahib," replied Imtiaz. "This Shakespeare play looks very good to me."

"Does it?" asked Mary Moses. "Well, I must think it through. We must consider the whole community, as well as the students, when we put on a play like this."

"Oh, the whole town will be liking it," said Imtiaz. "Have no fear of that." He smiled and left the room.

Mary Moses felt her headache deepening. She sighed and swallowed her aspirin with her tea. What Imtiaz had said was exactly what the problem was: Everyone would enjoy *As You Like It*. No one had a sense of responsibility any more. For a moment she felt deflated, disillusioned, as though someone had cut her strings to her God. She stood up impulsively, moved toward the telephone on the table, but then heard a rustle near the doorway. She put the phone down, went to the door, opened it, saw Alison standing there, about to speak.

Mary Moses tried to interpret the look in Alison's eye, as usual superior, certain. She decided then that maybe she should stop by the rehearsal that evening to see how things were going.

FLYING DOWN TO BOMBAY

From *The Times* of London: "After the ceremony, the Queen
appeared vastly amused when the frail, white-haired Sir Arthur,
in reply to her question, quipped, "I devoted my life to dance,
ma'am, because I was stolen away by some gypsies who forced
me into it for the money."

The man with the five gold rings on his hand swatted
Manookian smartly. "Stand over there," he said. "Stand up
straight."

Manookian did as he was told. They weren't going to hurt
him, he knew, but he couldn't figure out what they were up
to. He wondered why the left hand. He saw that one ring had
a diamond in the center of it.

The short woman hunched over the sewing machine
shouted out some words in Hindi to the ring man. Manookian
had no idea what she said, but the ring man beckoned to
Manookian, indicating that he should turn around in a circle.
Manookian did so. Both scrutinized him, and then the woman
went back to the sewing machine.

The ring man sat down on the charpoy where Manookian
had been sleeping before they prodded him to stand up in
front of them. Why were they measuring him? What was the
woman making at the sewing machine with that pile of black
cloth?

In a few minutes the woman grumbled something in an
indistinguishable Hindi again. The ring man shrugged, got off
the charpoy, went into an adjoining room, and returned with
a large stick, an ancient portable phonograph player, and a
few old records. He sat down on the floor, blowing dust off
the suitcase-like cover, opened the record player, blew some
more dust off the record itself, rubbed it with the palm of his
hand, and set the record on the turntable, carefully lowering

the tone arm on to it. He checked to see that it was cranked enough, and then delicately pushed the lever to start it. Manookian heard a far-off, tinny voice singing, "I'm puttin' on my top hat, tyin' up my white tie, brushin' off my tails." The man beat out the rhythm with the stick on the hard earthen floor.

The woman's eyes flashed some subliminal signal to the ring man. He shrugged again, but suddenly turned and swung out sharply at Manookian's shins with the stick. Manookian could tell that he wasn't aiming to hurt him or cripple him, that he wanted him to jump or move in some way. Manookian hopped. The man signaled with his eyes for Manookian to listen to the music. Did they want him to dance? He started a little dance. The man relaxed the stick. Both the man and the woman were smiling now, shaking their heads from side to side--*Atcha*! They wanted him to dance. They liked it when he did. That was easy.

Manookian last saw Saina, his ayah, at the train station in Bombay. She had left him just for a moment to go check on their reservations at the ticket counter. The next thing he knew, he found himself crowded in by this powerful man and this animal woman, who hustled him and his suitcase out into a waiting car, driven by someone they knew. He didn't have time to shout out or anything. The ring man said, "You are to come with us. Your father is our friend." Manookian, at first, thought that was the truth. He was to meet his father in New Delhi, and they must have known that he was traveling alone, air-conditioned first class, by train. But now, he realized, it had just been a lucky guess on their part.

Manookian was not Indian, but Armenian. He lived in London, but was in Bombay for the year with the whole family while his father expanded his business. It was spring holiday now and Manookian was to have visited a private school in New Delhi with his father. He would receive his main schooling at Eton when they returned to England next year.

Now the gypsies had stolen him away. He knew his mother would be distraught and would take to her bed. He knew Saina must be terrified. She was very nervous anyway, and was probably blaming herself for all this trouble. Manookian pictured her shrieking and wailing in his mother's bedroom. He knew his sister and brother would be wide-eyed, fascinated, and he could hardly wait to get home to tell them all about this wild adventure.

These people weren't hurting him, so he couldn't really complain. They seemed to be quite solicitous of him, in fact, making sure that he ate the dal and chapatties they brought him and drank the lemonade they made. And they didn't chain him up or otherwise mistreat him. He had a whole charpoy to sleep on, while they slept on the floor in one great lump under an old woolen blanket.

There was a little dog that kept barking just outside his window. The dog would run to the entrance and peer in anxiously at him from time to time. But it never entered the room. The rickshaw boys would hang out there, too, just outside the window. He could hear their laughter and the clink of their dice and coins. He could smell the pungent odor of their cigarettes, which he liked. Where was this place? Obviously some poor section of Bombay he had never been in before.

The woman wore a pale green and gold sari, tucked in at her waist. She worked her foot on the treadle of the sewing machine and glanced at Manookian every few minutes, sizing him up. She was making something for him, he knew. Then, on the third day, she brought into the room where he was an old, rolled-up poster. She flattened it out carefully, weighing it down with a bowl at one end, and her hand and the ring man's hand at the other. Manookian saw it upside down, but he could read what it said: "TOP HAT, starring Fred Astaire and Ginger Rogers." They both looked at him. He pointed to the poster and asked, "Fred Astaire?"

"Fred Astaire," the ring man said, smiling.

"Fred Astaire," the woman said in very uncertain English.

Manookian did a little dance, imitating the man on the poster.

They both smiled broadly and clapped their hands.

They seemd to relax with him now. The woman took the main body of the tailcoat out of the sewing machine. The arms weren't in it yet. She tried it on Manookian. It fitted perfectly. She seemed pleased, and then slipped one of the armpieces on him. The ring man said something to her. She pinched up the cuff a little, removed the armpiece, and went back to the sewing machine. The ring man indicated that Manookian should come, put both his hands on the poster in order to view it right-side up. The two males sat there in silence, looking at the image of the man and woman dancing in an elegant, romantic world.

The set of tails, complete with white tie, shirt, trousers, and black shoes was ready within the first week. The woman held up an old mirror in which Manookian could see his absurd reflection. He smiled. She smiled in return, as though to say, "Quite good, isn't it?" Every day now the ring man would bring out the record player and put on the record. Manookian would dance to it, catching the rhythm and jazz of it, looking out the corner of his eye to see what reaction he was getting from his captive audience. When they smiled, he knew that that move was just right. When they stared, he adjusted, changed his choreography, until he did something that pleased them. Each day they seemed more and more delighted with what he was doing. He did not think of home now. He concentrated on learning.

Then, in the third week, they indicated that he should follow them. They packed his suitcase with their things as well as his, picked up the record player and records, and drove away in the same car they had arrived in. Manookian sat in the car with his big black-olive eyes staring out the window, wondering where on earth they were going. Manookian was small for his age. He probably looked seven or eight, but actually he was ten.

They traveled for a long time until they came to the same Bombay railway station where they had first encountered him. Were they going to release him, then? He looked at them questioningly, but their eyes did not reveal any answers. They paid the driver, piled their belongings to one side in the shade, and motioned to Manookian to put on his little Fred Astaire outfit.

When he was dressed, they moved inside the station to a platform where a train was arriving from the south. As the gates were opened and streams of passengers flowed through, they put on the record while Manookian went into his *Top Hat* dance. Some people smiled and stopped, forming a large semi-circle around him. Others pushed right on past. After each dance, the audience applauded and the ring man took Manookian's top hat and collected money in it. Manookian danced five times for that train's arrival. One woman called out in English to the ring man, "Is that your son? What a little talent he is!" Manookian didn't answer.

Suddenly, there was a commotion and three or four police officers in khaki burst through the passengers and began beating the ring man with their clubs. The woman hastily grabbed at Manookian and tried to spirit him away, but the police nabbed her, too, while Manookian's jacket ripped as she was wrenched away from him. He found himself falling to the cold, polished floor of the station and he heard a desperate shout that he knew was the ring man's voice. When Manookian was lifted up again, he found himself in the arms of a police officer who was carrying him into a room in the railway station. He looked back to see where the ring man and woman were, but they had vanished, or else the police had taken them somewhere far from him.

The policeman set him down on a chair. He patted him on the head.

"We know who you are, Arthur Manookian," he said reassuringly.

Manookian sits in the big peacock chair on the veranda. He watches the mali dig in the rose garden. Mumtiaz brings him a glass of lemonade. His mother is playing the piano somewhere, and singing. His sister and brother are chasing the dachshund around near the gate. The garden is dappled in sunlight and shadow. Manookian has an empty notebook in his lap. He looks up at the clear blue sky and knows now what it is he wants to say. He writes in the book: "When I was captured by the gypsies was the first time in my life that I became a dancer."

A R G O S

They were going up a hill now, he could tell. He looked up from between the piles of coats and women where he was placed and tried to look around the chauffeur's cap in front of him. There was a quick blur of grey-green trees, like weeping willows, he thought, and then a swinging little turn in the road. Suddenly, the chauffeur blocked the view as he stopped the car, opened the door, and they all fell out, steadying themselves, pulling at their rumpled coats, bringing their sense of direction back into focus.

In front of him there was this immense stone building, cold, remote, not a castle, nor a home, perhaps a museum or library. His mother and his aunt Helen started in that direction. He followed.

"No," said his mother. "Stay here. See the pond." She pointed to the large pond carefully arranged in the landscape in front of the big building. She gestured vaguely toward the chauffeur, a gesture he understood to mean that the chauffeur should keep his eye on him. He had been in this situation many times before. Sometimes it was fun; othertimes it wasn't.

He ran over to the pond. It looked inviting. It was rimmed with glittery rocks set in concrete, forming a little railing all around it. You could lean on the rocks and not get your hands wet and muddy. Not bad. In the pond there were water hyacinths, green, pudgy, with long white tentacles hanging down, and in the dark water he saw huge goldfish flashing orange as they slithered their way from one hidden recess to the other and did vanishing acts among the tentacles. It was a bright, sunny day, and so all reflections were just perfect. He peered in at his own face, withdrawing a little when he saw the Eton cap and blue serge suit he was done up in. He took off his cap and put it by the side of the bench, also set in stone, so that it wouldn't blow away or get lost. He riffled the water with one hand to disturb the image, watching the little circular waves of reflection drift farther and farther away until the water became still once more.

Out of the corner of his eye, he knew the chauffeur was checking him out, watching so that he wouldn't do anything foolish and fall in. The chauffeur, he knew, was more interested in smoking a cigarette, as usual, and he could feel the chauffeur make quick, darting movements toward him and then away toward the gutter where he could more easily flick away the ash of his cigarette. The chauffeur always moved in this fast, angular pattern whenever he was freed from the long car.

He looked around now and saw that he was on the top of a high hill in the middle of the city. But the horizon had gone all green now, all willows and grass with huge white chess pieces studding the distant slope where there were also some flowers and people standing around. No children. Yes, there were two--a little boy and girl being pulled along with a tall man between them. The children looked unhappy. Who were they? Why were they sad? Didn't they see the pond with all those beautiful, shining goldfish dancing in it?

"You are to come with me now." He turned and saw the legs, shoes, pocketbook, and bottom part of his aunt's coat.

He didn't look up. The adults were not looking directly at him today, he had noticed.

"Don't want to," he said, riffling the water again, this time with a stick he had found, a nice pliable piece of willow.

"Walk with me," she said gently, so thoughtfully that he knew something was the matter, and so he turned full around to look up quickly at her face. Her eyes were troubled, he could tell; her voice was shaking just a little. Still, she smiled at him. She meant no harm. He would get up and walk with her.

"There are huge goldfish in the pond," he said.

"They are called koi," she told him. "I think they come from Japan."

"Oh," he replied. She took his hand. They walked a little around the pond. She squeezed his hand. He knew she was telling him something through this squeeze.

"Perhaps we shall get to Japan," she said. "Next year . . . perhaps. Would you like that?"

"Yes," he said, although he hadn't thought about it. He really just wanted to go to the lake in Connecticut again. That was such fun.

They walked in silence for a moment. They moved down a slanted path with gravel, going toward the far slope where the flowers, the people, and the big chess pieces were. The sun was very bright. His aunt stopped and shaded her eyes with the back of her hand as she looked deep into the distance. "We'll go back," she said, maneuvering him around on the path so that they were going uphill toward the great building again. Why did she hang on so tightly to his hand? He could move much better if she would let him go.

Now, down the steep steps of the big building came his mother in a great clutch of people, all dressed like her in dark clothes. They moved toward him until he was swallowed up again by adults twice as big as he. He couldn't see anything now but coats, suits, hands, and handbags. People were shaking hands and touching one another gently on the elbows, arms, shoulders. One or two people patted him

affectionately on the head, but they always did that. He put his
Eton cap back on so that it wouldn't happen again.

He knew they were avoiding looking directly at him for
some big reason, but he had to have one good look at his
mother's face. He saw pained eyes, sore from crying, a big
scar of a red mouth, whitened skin--and he knew at once her
terrible secret and why everybody was avoiding him: They
thought he was too young to know the meaning of these
important things. He looked down at the ground, holding on
tightly to his aunt's hand. She felt his tighter grip now, and he
could feel her looking down at him to discover whether he
had learned yet. He knew that his silence would tell her that
he had.

"Oreste," his mother said, almost bending down to his
level. "We shall go back to the car now." The clutch of
people moved toward the line of cars in their entourage,
sweeping him with them. The dapper chauffeur darted back
in front, swinging open the door of the car. Oreste climbed
into its sinister interior once more, seated again between his
mother and aunt, whose capacious coats flowed out from
them now, partly covering him with their warm textures and
floral aromas.

The chauffeur expertly jumped into the driver's seat, and
the car started off along the zig-zag downhill road again.
Suddenly, it stopped, and his mother leaned out. He saw great
stone pillars with intricate black iron gates swinging open,
and he saw a crowd of curious, ordinary people watching the
procession of cars as they exited from this special place out
into the maelstrom of life again. But what his mother was
leaning toward was a large man with uncommonly blue eyes,
curly grey hair and beard, who was holding an enticing flotilla
of balloons. He saw his mother hand the man a dollar,
drawing into the car a balletic pink balloon dancing at the end
of a string.

He was amazed. A Fourth-of-July surprise in the middle
of this heavy feeling. Was his mother smiling them? She was.
He thanked her and smiled back, feeling very pleased to hold

all this lightness on a string. He looked out at the man who had sold it to his mother, and he saw that the man, in the amplitude of his smile and the kindness of his eye, knew what it was that they had all come to this mysterious place for. He quickly averted his eyes, for he knew that his secret had to be not to let the grown-ups know that kids understand a lot too, sometimes more than other people would like them to know just yet.

As the long car pushed forward again through the crowd of babbling people trying to look into its smoked-glass interior, he noticed the name CYPRESS HILLS etched in the stone pillar.

He pulled the pink balloon down carefully toward his lap, and put it on short string, knowing that a thing so fragile and beautiful and light had to be handled very carefully when you are driving in a car through the city streets.

He knew that someday he would have to return to this place in search of an answer.

THE OYSTER WAGON

I knew they'd get the whole thing wrong, damn fools that they were, following the casket of that pompous General Keller which had just arrived at the station on the train from Manchuria. Singing, dancing, strutting their fool heads off, marching stridently to the booming sounds of an off-key military band dispatched by the magnificent Russian army to do the honors. It was a disgrace, I tell you.

I saw Anton Pavlovich's coffin before anyone else. It was dumped unceremoniously out of the box car into a God-damned green wagon with frayed, peeling paint, its narrow door insultingly marked OYSTERS in large letters. I saw the irony right away. It made me weep out loud in rivening gulps of despair. I immediately thought of a story he had written called "Oysters" back in 1884, the very year he received his medical degree. It was about an eight-year old boy so hungry that he fantasized eating anything to satisfy his hunger. When his father took him to a restaurant he saw the word "oysters" on the menu and said, "Papa, what does 'oysters' mean?" In the story, his father replied, "It is an animal that lives in the sea." Eventually, the boy tries to gobble up the oysters, shells and all, only to have the other diners laugh at him, but the father should have said "It's where your bones will come to rest, my son, among the creatures and detritus of the Black Sea in the hideous oyster wagon they will send for you, for that is the way your country will officially pay tribute to you."

So his followers originally thought the government had sent the brass band for him, and when they discovered the mistake, they thought it was funny, laughing and snickering like crazy hyenas. I realize it was a hot, dry day, with the dust flying up everytime you moved, but those idiots should have shown a little more respect.

A fat-guts police officer riding on a dirty white horse led the cortege from the station to the cemetery with the oyster wagon containing the body of that great subtle artist inside. I remember two avaricious lawyers skulking behind the wagon like selfish characters out of Gogol's *Inspector General*, probably unable to wait until they got their hooks into whatever part of the estate they could, and I heard that stupid man Maklakov talking about how clever poodle dogs were, standing on their hind legs, dancing in circuses, wearing skirts like ballerinas, and all. And there was this shrill lady in a purple dress with a lace parasol floating over her head jabbering on inanely about how witty Chekhov was, how charming, how clever--just the sort of thing that would have nauseated him. The man next to her countered by bragging about his dacha and the beauty of the Yalta countryside, especially the mountainside he lived on. I saw a few of my fellow actors from the theatre, but the whole scene was excessively vulgar and contradictory to the spirit of the man they thought they were honoring. So be it. That's the way life goes, isn't it? The supreme irony: Insensitivity. No one knew that better than Anton Pavlovich. That's why he called his plays comedies--human comedies--child-like adult beings unable to come to grips with reality, flitting from flower to bush to flower like butterflies, ephemeral, uncomprehending, but amusing to watch in a summer garden.

He was so different from me, calmer, I felt, although more fragile, yet he was a man I admired and loved. In his presence people automatically simplified themselves, became more honest. They knew that fancy phrases and literary airs wouldn't fool him. You must remember, he was first of all a doctor. He was trained to be impartial, non-judgmental, when it was needed. So he saw people with a dispassionate eye. In all his stories and plays you won't find him playing favorites. He was a tolerant, fair judge of men and women. He put me in my place the first time I ever read for him. "Now do it once again," he said, "and don't lie and posture this time."

He was cursed with that terrible ill health, of course. He had the same consumption that took his father and brother. He was only forty-four years old when he died. Sometimes you could see it in his eyes, gray they were, inwardly smiling, usually kind, although you could clearly see the early death gathering there at times and, in those moments, his eyes grew darker and harsher.

He went to Yalta for his health, but it didn't work. In the end, they had to haul him off to Badenweiler in Germany, but his damaged lungs finally gave out and he died in July, 1904, in that oafish land, surely another trick of the hellish fate in his life. God, when I think of that stinking wagon waiting for him at the railroad station in Moscow. Is this the way Russia honors its dead? A big parade for a jackass of a general; an oyster wagon for a great artist? Sometimes it is a disgrace to go on living if this is what it all comes to.

Well, I visited him several times in Yalta. His wasn't a large house, but it had a charming garden around it, a little brass plaque on the front door that read "A. Chekhov," an odd little bell that you twisted and it made a gentle ringing noise inside the house. The house was situated so that it fronted on the corniche with the back of it offering a view looking out to the sea. He loved to sit in the garden and stare far into the distance. Actually, the setting was quite Mediterranean. I think it reminded him of other places, of France, Italy, of the antique Arcady, perhaps. I don't really know. He moved there in 1898, and for a while he thought his health would improve and he would be safe.

The Yalta house was simple, functional, not designed to impress or fool anybody. There were no rugs on any of the floors. The furniture was massive and not particularly comfortable. Oh, of course, he had a good size desk, and just behind the desk there was a cozy alcove with a couch and a high window that gave a good light. When I visited the few times I was able to, I slept in the downstairs bedroom. His own bedroom upstairs was Spartan. There was always a kind of amber light in his room. I used to think it was the muses smiling beneficently on him. It certainly wasn't God. He also had an upright piano in the downstairs hall. Sergei Rachmaninoff played for Anton when he came to visit. Yes, even the great Count Leo Tolstoy came to see him sometimes, once when I was there. I remember meeting him--that great white beard and big hat. He and Anton Pavlovich would chat for hours.

I just recalled something odd. There were really no books to speak of in his house and nothing really theatrical, no posters or anything, which is curious since he was the rage of Moscow as a playwright and Olga created the dramatic role of Arkadina in *The Sea Gull*. But some theatre people are like that. I thought I was fairly severe in my own way of living, but my Moscow house was much more comfortable than anything Anton Pavlovich ever inhabited. Of course, he didn't marry Olga until 1901, and so they only had those last few years together. They were so often apart while she worked on the stage in Moscow.

The largest room in his Yalta house was the dining room, naturally, where we would gather around the table for good food and wine. He was always a thoughtful, considerate host, not only to me, but also to members of his family. He was proud of his brother, Nikolai, who was an illustrator, and almost all the paintings on the wall of his Yalta house were done by his sister, Maria. I remember she did a portrait of their mother who lived with him and had her own room. Maria's paintings were fairly crude and untutored, I always thought, but Anton Pavlovich was proud of them and displayed them instead of those by professional artists.

What kind of a God takes away a young artist at the height of his powers? Such a loss to the theatre, Russia, and the world. If only everyone realized that. I was twelve years younger and got to know him first when Constantine Stanislavsky was struggling to put *The Sea Gull* on at the Moscow Art Theatre in 1898. I played only a small part in that production, a mere servant that opened and closed doors, but it led to other parts--a Tolstoy play, a Gogol, and the great thing was that Vladimir Nemirovich-Danchenko approved of me also. I remember many French and Americans coming to see our work and we talked with them endlessly about the nature of art and the theatre. I don't think Constantine always made himself clear to them. Acting is always a fiction; it is never life itself. That is not what Stanislavsky said. It is simply seeming to be life-like. There is a difference.

Of course, there was a tug-of-war between Anton Pavlovich and Constantine. All those crickets chirping off stage. "Too much," said Anton Pavlovich. He was right. You can only go so far in creating realism. You don't need to overpower the audience with realistic-seeming effects. Leave something to the actors, to nuances, to the silences. And that's why I think the second *Sea Gull* was a huge success while the first production in St. Petersburg in 1896 had been a dismal failure with the audiences laughing their fool heads off. Nobody stopped ever. There were no pauses. Everyone spoke in a clippity-clop fast-paced style the way they did in the English theatre.

No, there is a deep-sea current in Anton Pavlovich's plays, and that was Constantine's and Vladimir's great discovery--the inner life. All they did was bring this out through their actors--and that made everything seem truthful and right. But that's what art does or should do.

I am older now. I sit in gardens in parks sometimes and watch people as they pass by, observing quietly how they walk, how they laugh, how they notice or don't notice. I can detect when a person is in love. I see serious purpose in some business people's strides. I yearn to reach out to those who are ill or forgetful. I laugh openly when a child finds something delightful or amusing, like trying to catch a pigeon or chasing a squirrel that dodges up a tree. I try to look at life with Anton Pavlovich's eyes, but only his really see the foolishness, the frivolity, and the beauty of life with all its frittering away. I see too much the sadness. I dream too much of the past.

You know, about a year before we put on *The Cherry Orchard* at the Moscow Art Theatre, I remember Anton Pavlovich showing me a draft of it in Yalta and I dared to ask him if there was a part in it for me. He smiled understandingly, and I could see amusement dancing in his eyes. "There's something for you, Petya," he said. "You will find yourself there. There's something for all actors in this new play."

He was right. I don't think I have ever been more excited in the theatre than I was when we played *The Cherry Orchard* in Moscow in January, 1904. I played the part of an intense university student named Petya Trofimov and stood in the wings waiting for my cue while watching first Lopahin, the merchant, and Dunyasha, the maid, scurrying about on stage in preparation for the arrival of Madame Lyubov Ranevskaia and her brother, Gaev, who have been away in Paris for five years where they fled after her little son Grisha accidentally drowned in the pond. You can imagine how anxious my character felt because I had been the little boy's tutor. Next, Epihodov, a clerk, enters the stage with a nosegay of flowers, then, suddenly, there is the clattering of two off-stage horse-drawn carriages pulling up in front of the house; everyone rushes off and the stage is empty for a long moment as one hears the excited shouts and greetings of

Gaev and Lyubov returning to their childhood home. The ancient servant, Firs, crosses the stage and goes tottering out to greet his charges. The anticipation is overwhelming. It courses through the audience like lightning, to the actors involved in the off-stage bustle, to me waiting for my cue to enter.

Finally, the suspense is broken. In a breathless rush, Lyubov Ranevskaia makes a dramatic quick entrance, taking everything in, rushing to the window of the room that was once her nursery, looking out toward the famous cherry orchard that she will say goodbye to at the end of the play as, "My life, my youth, my happiness." She is followed by her daughters, Anya and Varya, her brother, Gaev, and Charlotta Ivanovna, the governess, cradling a dog in her arms. And in that magical moment, with everyone on stage laughing and crying with joy and sorrow for the lost years in Paris, I make my entrance, kiss Lyubov's hand while she clasps me close to her as we think of the soul of little Grisha. At the end of the First Act, I look at her beautiful daughter Anya, whom I love, and say, "My sunshine, my spring." And in the Second Act, I have long speeches in which I talk philosophically about the past, present, and future of Russia. Only once in a blue moon does an actor have someone write a part for him as great as this one is. That's the kind of man Anton Pavlovich was. He gave me the gift of lifting me out of life and putting me into his play.

I gave many performances in *The Cherry Orchard* over the years. I played Petya Trofimov as long as I could, only as I grew older I gradually became Lopahin, then Gaev, and finally Old Firs. No matter what the part, I always thought of that ugly green oyster wagon as I entered the stage, and I'd want to kill someone for what they did to him, but I always brought my real thoughts under control, for that's what acting is, and I'd go on to play my part the way he wrote it in the most beautiful play ever created for the Russian theatre. In my curtain calls, you'd always find me smiling because I reached out to a place far beyond the audience, above it and the applause, with the thanks that only a grateful actor can give to the one who gave him life and a reason for being.

Rachmaninoff Blues

If you ask me, I'll tell you officially that I don't believe in reincarnation and think Hinduism, Shirley MacLaine, astrology, and spiritual advisors are all a giant crock. Even the toughest of ghosts lives on only in transient memory. But the plain truth is that when I was ten I was Frederic Chopin living in a villa on the edge of the Mediterranean and my best friend was Sergei Rachmaninoff. This is a little-known interior fact about me.

Sometimes I can still feel the ancient deep sea current that runs through my life. It initially reached me when I was very young, its vibrations widening to carry me to a larger world of intelligence and beauty, but, then, having touched it, I let it go, or so I thought. I pressed on, settling for surfaces, shiny little flashes of silver that flickered just in front of me.

First, I finished law school, then clerked for a Supreme Court justice in Washington, then swam to Covington & Burling. After that, it was time for New York and a wife, an apartment, a beach house in Westhampton, and a couple of kids. I gave generously to the arts and all good causes, but I see now that the world I inhabit is really one of reflected mylar images, answering machines, faxes, and computers, where restaurants replace art and television replaces intellect. I wonder every day at the image I see in my mirror. Who is that man? Only rarely do I remember the time when I had a friend named Hartley and life was something mysteriously glowing ahead of us, like a distant magical shore we both knew could provide joy in its very discovery.

Maybe I went there in the first place because I was curious to see who lived in that exotic salmon-colored Spanish hacienda. I was only ten and a classic villa with a red-tiled Mediterranean roof on our plain little island in Maine suggested romance and adventure to me. My piano teacher had to be somebody unusual to live in an imaginative place like that. I pictured her as George Sand and me as a possible Frederic Chopin, she inspiring, and I composing all day, squeezing all the genius and beauty out of me before I would die of the tuberculosis I was convinced I had. I knew in advance all about artistic creation and life on Majorca. After all, I was obviously destined for music. My soul was fairly oozing with it. My arms and hands wanted to express it. I drummed my fingers on anything that resonated. Something simply had to be done about it, said my mother, the organizer, and my father, the arts advocate. Piano lessons seemed to be the perfect answer.

To those New England neighbors who looked askance at such extravagant ambition in a simple boy, my parents explained pragmatically that I had shown "unusual receptivity to music." They threw in veiled references to Mozart, as though that would impress anybody, which it didn't. But what did my family care, anyway? The neighbors knew us as reckless Bohemians holed up on the island with our mother and our father, a highbrow college professor who showed up on week ends from Cambridge. Besides, they were convinced I was spoiled.

Maybe I was. I had already made a false start in music. When I was in the second grade, a genuine Italian maestro, recently furloughed from the Boston Symphony, came to our island to teach children how to play the violin. "The younger, the better," he said. What an impressive sight he was with a bristling mustache, a full head of tossed black hair, a relentless glare in his eyes, and a ramrod posture that let you know he meant business. I took lessons long enough to have my photo taken with violin in hand, looking as though I were about to pluck the hell out of it as I had the piano, Maestro glowering in the background like some avenging Paganini about to swoop down on an inept pupil, but when I burst into tears and fled from school in despair one day, my parents took pity on me and said maybe the violin was not quite the right instrument for me.

For a while, nothing further was said or done about music. But in a house where my father sang opera while shaving in the morning and my mother played show tunes on our Steinway grand, music was bound to erupt in my burgeoning soul again. And so it did. It crept in when the house was empty and the possibilities for self-expression were at their fullest. I would slip to the piano, lift up the lid, prop it up to its highest point, and strum the long strings inside the shiny black wooden body. I could get harp-like sounds out of it, strange, twanging notes, vibrations from other planets and unseen galaxies. My sister, Jenny, and my little brother, Harpo, the born fool, caught me doing this one day and told my parents I was banging and ruining the piano. But my father said I was creating an original art form, and that shut them up, you can bet. Shortly after, my parents announced that I would be taking piano lessons from Eleanor Loring, whom my mother knew from the Congregational Ladies' Aid Society. Mr. Loring sang tenor in the church choir, my mother told me, and had a voice worthy of the Metropolitan. Piano lessons were my parents' birthday present to me that year. I could hardly wait.

Eleanor Loring, as it turned out, was born to disappoint all sybaritic ten-year olds. She most closely resembled the hickory coat rack that stood guard duty in our downstairs hall. Tall, thin, smelling vaguely of colonic irrigation which she took religiously, she was a tolerant but unamusing Calvinistic piano teacher of the old school. Where I might have looked for imagination, she offered technique. This meant the Thompson-Hanon-Czerny route, and no nonsense about it. But if it took practicing three hours a day and giving up baseball with my friends who thought I was the living

56

definition of left field, then so be it. Mrs. Loring was to be my guide at least to the top of the earthly paradise.

It wasn't easy. Little penances loomed up all along the way. One I particularly remember was that at my weekly lesson every Saturday morning, I would have to sit next to Mrs. Loring at the old upright she used for teaching, feet firmly planted on the rubber mat she placed beneath the pedals "to ward off the danger of being struck by lightning during a thunderstorm," as she put it.

The really enticing thing about Mrs. Loring was her nephew, Hartley, who came with his feisty grandmother to stay with the Lorings every summer from their home in Vermont. Mrs. Loring would talk about him all the time which made me think I was being compared unfavorably to him. He was supposed to be this child prodigy, but he sounded more like a spoiled brat to me, and I began hating him, the more she bragged about him. I guess she eventually sensed the topic was boring to me, so she dropped it, thank God, and let me move at my own meticulous pace at the piano.

One Saturday morning, as I approached her house, I heard this incredible music coming from it. I didn't know Mrs. Loring could play so well. This was strong music, full of passion, color, and excitement. I looked through the screen door and saw her standing over a hunched-over figure with arms flailing away like Rubenstein in full concert. Wouldn't you know it was the genius nephew. And wouldn't you know I was dead wrong about this kid.

Hartley was a year older than I, oddly put together like some puppety Pinocchio, tall, thin, double-jointed all over, but he talked a blue streak and was astonishing at the piano. He had already been declared a genius in Vermont so that he was studying with the best teachers there and there was talk of sending him down to the Curtis Institute in Philadelphia next year, by-passing the New England Conservatory of Music, which, I gathered, was not considered sufficient to contain his talent. He and his aunt had a kind of agreement about musical technique--no countermanding or undermining of each other's approach to the art. Rarely did they share information or divulge trade secrets. With the wide bridge of his hands and his percussive fingers, Hartley attacked the piano like some wild hurricane boiling up out of the Atlantic. He was constantly inventing and imitating. I heard him play Mozart in a dissonant, balletic style, Bach as progressive jazz, Beethoven as barrelhouse. I could toss out a composer's name to him, and there he would be, snatching sounds out of the air, scaring the daylights out of me with his intense ingenuity. Beloved of God was Hartley indeed!

That first day was extraordinary, the kind of day you realize years later marked a turning point. For me, Hartley's arrival was a confirmation of the importance music was to have in my life. I linked it with the first time I had ever heard Frederic Chopin's music. I was in the hospital recovering from a feverish pneumonia that almost did me in. The nurse had turned on the small radio next to my bed on a Sunday morning and I heard this distant, tinkling, unearthly music, so intriguing that I turned it up to hear the commentator explain all about Chopin's life, how he was this thin, neurasthenic Pole nursed by a caring woman whimsically named George Sand on the island of Majorca. I immediately identifed with the forlorn Frederic, a poor, wan youth whose genius would have to be encouraged by some unknown woman to come, certainly not by Nurse Ratched, my nurse, but maybe it could be Mrs. Loring, or by indirection, her nephew if he played the piano like this. I thought I was looking for a goddess, but maybe it was a god instead.

That first day, I had no lesson at all. It was completely usurped by Hartley. His aunt and I listened as he gave us an impromptu concert and a running commentary on it. He knew so much, he was bursting with talent, he was unlike any of my other friends, unlike any other human being on the island. After about an hour, Mrs. Loring dismissed us, saying maybe Hartley could accompany me on my walk back home since he wouldn't stop talking and was curious to meet someone his own age.

We crossed through the woods, Hartley having finished with Bach and now rhapsodizing about Mozart. We were just in sight of Cobb's pond when a huge bird flapped in for a noisy, splashy landing on the dark blue water. Hartley scared me by screaming and grabbing my arm and throwing me to the ground.

"What's that?" he whispered, frightened.

"A blue heron," I replied. "You see them once in a while."

"Look at that," he said, pointing at a deer standing stock still by a tree at the far end of the pond, quietly focusing his attention on the disturbance in the water.

"Oh, yeah. The deer are mostly back there in the woods and in the meadow in the center of the island. They like the pond, but I usually only see them here in the morning mists or just before dark. You'd better get up. The deer and mice have ticks here. They carry Lyme disease."

"What's that?"

"I don't know. I think it twists your face and your brain. I've only heard about it. I think it makes you tired, too. My mother knows someone who has it."

"Listen. Are those crickets chirping?"

"No. We call them peepers. Summer's here."

"Where do you learn this stuff?"

"It's just science. My father's a geologist."

You're smart. Do you know that?" said Hartley. "Do you like living here year-round?"

"It's okay," I replied. "We go to Boston sometimes, too. My grandparents live there."

"My grandma thinks people who live on islands are batty. She says Aunt Eleanor is a fool to put up with it for her husband's sake."

"Why would she say that?" I asked. "An island is a whole world."

"No. Music is a whole world. An island is just a little world."

One morning I was late getting to my summer job at the boathouse. I was surprised to see Hartley among the crowd of tourists on the wharf because I'd stopped by Mrs. Loring's house twice that week only to have his nagging grandma chase me off by telling me he was practicing and couldn't be disturbed. I had decided that music was also like a prison, shutting you off from friends, sunlight, and good times.

"What are you doing here?" I asked Hartley, relieved to see he hadn't rejected me completely.

"I needed a break," he said. "I wanted to see what you do."

"I shovel people onto the ferry and ship them back to the mainland," I replied. "But I'm late." I rushed off.

"I discovered something really interesting today," he shouted after me. "Come by the house later?"

"Okay," I said, jumping on the boat because I could see Old Sims' evil eye focusing on me telling me to haul ass and get to work. He indicated two ancient grand dames, one on a cane, hobbling up the gangplank. I rushed over to offer assistance.

After lunch, which ran late because Old Sims sent me out on some fool delivery, I spotted Tim Hauser shoving off in his snipe, so I hitched a ride with him. He lived next to the Lorings, just across the cove. Tim was the pitcher for our baseball team. He had the best arm on Spanish Island. I saw him studying me.

"Heard you found a new friend," he said,"That queer kid from Vermont. What'd you want to hang out with him for?" He smiled.

"I like music."

"Brad Lewis likes music, too. He's getting up a band."

"Good music," I emphasized.

"Brad plays electric guitar. Maybe you could do keyboards."

"Never mind," I said.

I was anxious to reach shore now. I was sorry I had sailed with Tim. I thought it would be a quicker way to get to Hartley. I wanted to see what he had to show me. But the wind had died now. The single sail hung limp against the spar. We weren't going anywhere.

"You coming back to practice?" Tim asked.

"Don't know. Maybe."

"I guess you'd rather play church music, huh?"

"Shut up, Tim. You know nothing about it."

"Look at that," Tim said, making sucking noises at some older girls in bright bikinis sunbathing on the rocks. Naturally, they ignored us, but I know they recognized us.

"You wanna catch pneumonia?" Tim shouted, pulling on the tiller as though he were going to spin the snipe around. We drifted by them ineffectually.

"Come on, Tim," I snapped. "Could we just get to your pier?"

We sat in silence for a while. I now saw Tim for what he was--truly inferior compared with my new friend, but I realized there were many Tims and only one Hartley in my world. It made me depressed.

I noticed Joe Carter walking along the beach with his golden retriever when suddenly he picked up a piece of silver driftwood and hurled it far out in our direction. The dog jumped into the dark blue water and began swimming toward us.

"Look at that," shouted Tim. "Come on, Chauncey. Swim. Come on, boy."

"He's faster than this boat is," I said. "Why don't you use the paddle?"

Chauncey turned back, the driftwood secure in his mouth, and swam furiously through the cold water to shore. Above him, on the cliff, I noticed a crew setting up a white canopy tent on the Carters' sloping green lawn in preparation for Gemma Carter's wedding tomorrow, the big social event of the summer season. The gardener was busy studding their flower beds with store-bought geraniums and pink petunias.

Across the cove, seeming far away and unattainable, I could see the red-tiled roof of the Loring villa looming up on the point. I thought we would never get there with the slow-motion wind and the fussy little tacking maneuvers Tim was making.

I leaned back in resignation, thinking how perfect Hartley was and how little Tim really knew. I used to admire Tim, but Hartley was obviously better. He was an artist, an ideal human being, and that's what I wanted to be--not some total idiot like Tim. I let my hand trail in the water, feeling wise, superior, but betrayed by Tim the Dumb and his ilk. Then suddenly the wind picked up, a wake rippled out around us, and the sail blossomed out. I could feel the current coursing through my fingers, at first weak, but then steadier. We surged forward strongly, aiming straight for the world of intelligence and beauty in that magical Spanish hacienda, or so it seems to me now so many years later.

"Almost there," Tim said.

After we reached shore, I helped Tim tie up the snipe. I climbed the wooden stairs from the Hausers' landing to their house and then crossed over to the Lorings' place. Hartley was sitting in his aunt's back yard, a large book open on his lap. "Look at this," he said, showing me a photograph.

"Who is it?"

"Sergei Rachmaninoff. Notice anything?"

"Like what?"

"Look at me."

I searched Hartley's face.

"Don't you see it? The resemblance? That's the way I'll look when I'm thirty." He was excited. He flipped over a page. "Read that."

"Sergei Rachmaninoff was born in Nizhni-Novgorod, Russia, April 2nd, 1873."

Hartley closed the book with a snap. "That's my birth date too," he said. "April 2nd."

"So?"

"There's more. Here's another photograph of Rachmaninoff's hands, a close-up of them at the piano. Look. His fingers and the bridge of his hands are almost identical to mine."

"They are?"

He spread out both his hands like two twisted seagulls in flight. I saw the unusually wide bridges and the stretch of skin and bones that held his strong hands together so that he could cover vast distances at the keyboard with one span.

"Listen to this," I said, reading the text under the photo. "It says that Rachmaninoff died in Beverly Hills, California on March 28th, 1943. I thought he was Russian."

"He was, but he ended up here. He went to California for his health. Do you realize he began studying at the conservatory at age nine?" said Hartley. "That's just the age I was when I began at my conservatory. I'm learning all his music now. It's very difficult, but somehow it comes easily to me."

"Does this mean you will die in Beverly Hills on the same day he did?"

"Maybe," Hartley said. "I'd like to go to California, to Paso Robles where he lived. But I can't go now because my father lives there, and I won't see him. No one in my family will."

I noticed that his eyes darkened and he seemed angry. I quickly changed the subject back to Rachmaninoff. "Well, I think someday you'll be as famous as him," I said.

"Who?"

"Rachmaninoff."

"That's what I want more than anything else in the world," he said with an intensity so fierce it frightened me. "And you, Patrick, what will you be when you grow up?" He slammed the photograph album shut with a finality as though that would end the subject and headed toward the house, I trailing along in his wake.

The implications of his question didn't hit me just then and I almost blurted out that I wanted to be a pianist too, but I realized he wouldn't believe I had the proper sort of dedication. Like Tim, he probably saw me as a dabbler, who took up music or baseball, depending on my mood, a whistler in the wind, which I was afraid I was. After all, everybody I knew always said about anyone interested in music, art, or literature, "What are you going to do with it?" That, and a little laugh always went together. How could I have had any confidence in myself, especially when compared to the giant talent of Hartley? Mozart, Beethoven, Rachmaninoff were beyond my grasp. However, I sincerely thought I could aim for the second rung of musicians--Chopin, Mendelssohn, Grieg. But wouldn't the brilliant Hartley also put me down if I dared say "Chopin" to him?

"Maybe I could teach kids someday, the way your aunt does," I said, thinking it a very practical answer, and his glance seemed to indicate acceptance of it, "if I live that long," I added.

"What do you mean?"

"Well, I almost died once of pneumonia and I'm sure I'll get tuberculosis sooner or later."

Hartley hooted. "No one gets tuberculosis anymore, Patrick. Chopin died of it. But they can cure it now."

He had used the name of my idol. Had he guessed my intention and thought me a complete fool? I'm sure I blushed. "Maybe so," I said. "Anyway, if I have good health, then I think I can do almost anything I want."

"That's what Aunt Eleanor says, '"If your health is good, the world is good.' You know, you're really very wise, Patrick."

Hartley went into the house, leaving me out in the cold once more. I was so mad, I stormed away thinking I'd go to baseball practice with Tim and company again, but when I got home, what to my wondering eyes did appear, but Harpo the born fool perched at the piano like some demented bird, pecking away in a satiric imitation of me, I was sure. I forced him to vacate not only the room, but the house, and I took over, practicing for two and a half hours until my mother came home and stood in the doorway with an alarmed Harpo and Jenny staring at me as though I had gone mad. I shut the piano lid deftly, not telling anyone of my resolve. I ate my dinner in stony, concentrated silence, returned to the piano after dinner and practiced for another two hours until Harpo shouted down that he couldn't get to sleep. I decided then that Hartley could end up as Mr. Beethoven or Mr. Sergei Rachmaninoff reincarnated, but I secretly would become the dying Chopin, eking out slim, quiet melodies on a solitary piano despite what Hartley and the world may have thought of me, or maybe because of what they thought. This was heady stuff I was wading into the summer of my tenth year.

Each summer after that at the beginning of June, Hartley would come over on the ferry from the mainland to stay with his aunt and uncle. Each year Mrs. Loring would prepare me to play something on the piano especially for Hartley so that he could assess my progress. He liked my Grieg, thought less of my Debussy, said I showed some fire in my Liszt. I could tell I wasn't winning, though, or even gaining, and so I decided to try to integrate Hartley into my circle of friends because I really missed baseball which I was pretty good at, and, besides, we needed another man in right field. But Hartley tried to analyze the game, was over-protective of his fingers, and was annoyed at the lack of interest in art and intellectual matters among my friends. "Geniuses in a hurry have little time for ordinary minds and matters," explained my father. My gang simply saw Hartley as another white-faced summer visitor from Oz.

Hartley was not just a music freak. He had developed other interests. He liked walking, which he did at a very fast clip when he took breaks from practicing the piano. These walks brought out an extraordinary scientific curiosity in him, which he may have gotten from me. He observed birds, butterflies, insects, plants, animals, trees--all the natural things as we walked, and he would ask me questions about them, which flattered me, as though I knew all.

"What's that purple flower?"

"Loosestrife."

"What's that slimy mold on the rocks?"

"That's not mold. They're lichens."

"What's a lichen?"

"Part fungus, part algae."

His interest did not stop with easy answers. He did further research in his aunt's books and in the library. He collected and mounted some moths and butterflies, becoming almost the island's leading authority on them in a single summer. He made an unusual collection of insects that made scraping sounds with their legs and wings, like grasshoppers and locusts, and pinned them on velvet-covered cardboard in glass cases. "Insects have a music of their own," he announced. "Listen. Hear them singing in the meadow? Their music isn't pleasant; they scream, sing off key, and warn human beings that they will get them."

Hartley disdained city stuff—especially concrete, man-made structures of any kind, and whizzing vehicles, including fast boats and airplanes. Anything made of plastic or aluminum earned his instant scorn, and when he saw refuse wash up on the rocks from the sea, he lectured me on oil companies and sloppy fishermen as though I personally were responsible for all pollution in the ocean. He had the musician-scientist's passion for accuracy and perfection. My father said Einstein and Schweitzer were the same way. My father also said Hartley was so far above my other friends it wasn't funny.

The summer when I was thirteen and Hartley fourteen, he said he was going to play something incredibly difficult but exciting on our Steinway just for us. He arrived with his aunt, whom he said was to be a silent witness and venture no opinions, just listen to our reactions. We gathered around and listened as he soared through passages of strong contrast and heady emotions, passionate arpeggios, dazzling runs up the scale, reminding me of thunderclouds and hurricanes racing in from the sea. "What was that music?" I asked when he finished.

"The first two of Rachmaninoff's *Etudes Tableaux*," he said. "I'm learning them now."

"Magnificent," said my father.

"Hartley, that's so beautiful," said my mother. "Your technique, your range is phenomenal."

"Did you like it?" Hartley asked, hunkering down to look at little Harpo face-to-face.

"It was sad," Harpo said. "It scared me, too."

"I thought it was very dramatic," Jenny said in her phony know-it-all artistic voice that made Hartley turn red so that I shot her a dirty look.

Then, suddenly, Harpo was tugging at Hartley's sleeve. "Did your mother really get killed by a car?" he asked. There was an instant freeze in the room. Mrs. Loring stiffened and closed the lid on the piano. Hartley looked trapped.

"Shut up, Harpo," I said, although I too had heard the story and had always wanted to ask Hartley about it.

"We have to go," Mrs. Loring said, giving Mom a pale smile. "Thank you for letting us come."

After they left, Harpo caught polite hell from Mom who said he lacked discretion, which didn't faze him; he didn't know what discretion was. He explained that Hartley was the only person he knew whose mother was dead. I had to admit that he was honest about that.

Hartley had always seemed to me to have a certain *tristesse* lurking around him, even when he made jokes. In my mind I linked up the dark colors of the new Rachmaninoff music with this underlying melancholy. I sensed that it had to do with Hartley's parents, particularly with his mother, who had been Mrs. Loring's sister, Eugenia. I kept thinking about it and one evening when we were out moth hunting and talking the way you do when it's night and you tell all your secret feelings to friends, I asked, "Why won't you talk about your mother, Hartley. I mean, I know

Harpo's a brat, but I've heard that story too and wondered if it were true."

"It's true."

"I'm sorry."

"It's okay. It happened when I was a baby. My mother was hit by a car while she was carrying me across the street."

"How terrible."

"I got some cuts and bruises. I don't remember it. Grandma does."

"What about your father?"

"What father? He divorced my mother. I never saw him. He didn't even come to the funeral. I hate him. I hate him so much."

I'd heard about his father, too, but only that he had remarried and lived in California and had an uninteresting job in computers. At any rate, he was not a musician, and neither Hartley nor his aunt ever spoke about him. His name was Walter Skeuse, I had heard. Hartley's real name was Walter Hartley Skeuse, but he was always called Hartley so far as I knew and lived most of the year with his maternal grandmother and grandfather in Vermont. This mystery about Hartley made him all the more appealing to me, the romanticism of a tragic artistic life. An ill-fated Chopin like me well understood the sensitivity of enigmatic persons like Hartley. I was discreet enough not to inquire further at that time, but my curiosity was permanently aroused and always sought for elusive clues.

One summer Hartley didn't appear. Too busy, his aunt told me, studying, preparing for that concert pianist's career God and he were designing for him. This spurred me on to practicing all the harder that summer. But the next summer I was seventeen and when Hartley didn't show up I realized he would probably never come to the island again.

Mrs. Loring was losing all patience with me now. I was branching out in ways she didn't like--playing rock music with Brad Lewis' band, calling the piano "keyboards," fooling around with guitars and synthesizers. Worse, I was composing in this new style. She said all rock was "so many insects clacking away" and that the Beatles were appropriately named as was Mick Jagger who she said had evidently crawled out from under a non-rolling stone. She said my singing voice sounded "adenoidal" and the songs I was composing were "mumbo-jumbo." She told my mother I had gone off the deep end. Proof positive, she said, was my long hair, the earring in my ear, and the bizarre ads on my tee-shirts.

But, while I was on a downward slide, Harpo, the born fool, was in the ascendant, playing Chopin's "Polonaise in A-Flat Major" to Mrs. Loring's and everybody else's huge satisfaction. Mrs. Loring's piano recitals had now become main events on the island and Harpo became her star performer. I was never invited to appear. I was too risky, she told my parents. It was my look, my aberrant technique, my dangerous tendency to improvise, to break into what she referred to as "something uncalled for, something not quite music" that made me pianist *non grata.*

She needn't have worried. I learned plenty from her. I still respected Debussy and Satie; in fact, I openly imitated them, but I liked all the new sounds I heard too. What an orgy of self-expression I had booming out through amplifiers and speakers. I as star performer with a great big voice, swagger, and sound, backed up by twanging, thwacking friends on drums, bass, and guitar. I knew I ran the risk of the old Salieri-Mediocrity show, but what the hell. I was growing up, moving into some kind of outer-galactic orbit. Sometimes I thought cynically of Hartley and old Rachmaninoff aging together, creating turbulent sounds that competed and clashed with mine, but Hartley was not in my life anymore and neither was Rachmaninoff.

One night at Dartmouth we were boozing it up in the fraternity house, being particularly polite and decorous so the neighbors wouldn't complain, when a telephone call came for me. It was my mother.

"Harpo called and said that Mrs. Loring gave him some good news about Hartley today. I thought you'd be interested." Usually, when she called, she included the latest bulletin about Hartley that Harpo, the crack pianist, had gotten from Mrs. Loring.

"What about him?"

"He just won a major piano competition in Vienna."

"Great."

"Mrs. Loring says he will make his European debut there and after that will play in Paris. She herself is arranging his New York debut. She hopes to get Carnegie Hall."

"Wonderful. Send me the reviews. Keep me posted."

"Harpo played in Bangor last Sunday. Everybody just raved about his playing. He did Debussy's *La Cathedrale Engloutie*. Remember all the trouble you had with it?"

"Give him my best."

I celebrated Hartley's victory, and Harpo's, in what I considered an appropriate style. After I had finished quite a few drinks, I sat down at the piano in my moodiest manner and banged out a few old Rachmaninoff rags of my own. Memory is the joint I always stumble to when I want to sing the blues. I moved from quiet, slim, sensitive themes of youthful innocence into full-blown cadenzas and agitatos in the grand Romantic style worthy of old friend Hartley, idiot savant Harpo, and old fart Rachmaninoff. Unfortunately, the window behind me was open and the dumb neighbors called to complain. "Tell them I'm playing the "Rachmaninoff Blues," I shouted to the guy who answered the phone. Then I quit and slammed down the lid of the piano angrily, wishing I could get inside that hateful instrument and pluck the steely strings out of its treasonable heart.

Naturally, the next day, I conveniently forgot all about it and went back to plodding the established trail to law school where all the surrendered writers, actors, artists, and musicians of the world eventually end up.

Ten years later. Zurich, 1985: We were staying at the Baur au Lac. We had just flown in from Venice. My wife, Kerry, was anxious to meet the famous concert pianist of my New England youth. So were our children. They had heard his moving recording of the *Etudes Tableaux* which Mrs. Loring had sent to me via Harpo one Christmas. I called on the telephone. Liselotte, his wife, answered. Yes, they knew that we were coming. Yes, it is not far. Just this way and that. In an hour we arrived and a door opened suddenly. A rush of greetings. A huge Hartley, looking like an intellectual television wrestler, gave me a giant bear-hug and my wife a sloppy kiss. We were in a small room with two pianos, a Bechstein and a Steinway, a harpsichord, with stacks of music piled up to the ceiling, and a voluble red and blue parrot swinging crazily on a perch in its cage over the Bechstein.

Hartley, grown older, slightly grey, and corpulent now, boomed out heartily at my children. "Let's see. Now you are Elissa, right? And you must be Miss Maggie. Well, I think we need a merry, laughing tune for Elissa, and for Miss Maggie, I think a whole hillside of Scottish heather and the sound of the pipes is called for." And he took off at the piano, focusing all his genius now into these improvisations for my daughters, sending up flower gardens of beauty and happiness into the room. The children and Kerry were enchanted. I was propelled back into the past. I couldn't believe the physical transformation of the thin stringbean Hartley into this huge bear-like Hemingway of a man. Liselotte, a Degas-like dancer, sat on the floor in open admiration, taking everything in. She knew of those early summers in Maine. She knew how happy this reunion was for Hartley and me.

"Patrick," Liselotte said in her husky voice, her grey eyes luminous with happiness. "What was he like, the truth, as a boy? Was he difficult?"

"No," I said. "He was incredible--inventive, imaginative. He set me on fire."

"Did he do that?" Liselotte teased, poking her arm into her enormous husband.

"No, I couldn't have," Hartley said, turning red.

"I accepted Hartley as Rachmaninoff," I replied. "Nobody, not even Sergei himself, could have played his music more movingly."

"But you played, too," interrupted Hartley. "Do you still . . ?"

"I wanted to be Chopin for a while," I said, laughing. "Do you remember that? Then, later, Grieg or Mendelssohn. It kept diminishing until now I play only some popular music, some rock music maybe, nothing important."

"But you also play jazz," said Kerry. She whispered to Liseleotte. "He plays quite good fusion jazz."

"Jazz is good," said Liselotte, "but rock is noise. It is so many insects squeaking."

"That's what your aunt used to say," I said, looking at Hartley. "This could open up a nasty subject."

Hartley put his arm on his wife's shoulder. "Sweetheart, no lectures, please. Patrick is blessed. He has a career, a lovely wife, children, and good health, as you can see. I have only a little art left." Hartley turned and smiled at me that dazzling, expansive Rachmaninoff smile. Did he remember too?

Kerry looked around the crowded living room. "Your apartment is wonderful," she said. "Anyone would realize that interesting people live here." Maybe, I thought, but it was obviously a small living room, kitchen, and one bedroom--crammed to the gills with books, music, programs--hard to find a couch, a chair--like an overgrown office or studio, the kind of severe space all artists everywhere inhabit, understand, and grow to love.

After dinner, Liselotte took Kerry and the children out to see the garden and the view from the headland overlooking Lake Zurich. Hartley and I walked a little apart from them. We chatted amiably about my mother and Harpo's musicianship, and then I asked him something that had been puzzling me. "Why are you billed now as Walter Skeuse? What happened to Hartley?"

He stopped and looked at me in surprise. "I thought you knew," he said. "I supposed aunt Eleanor had told you."

I shook my head, but did not tell him that his aunt had never mentioned him at all in the years prior to her death.

"Do you remember the story of my mother's early death, how she was hit by a car when I was still a baby?"

"Yes."

"It wasn't true. She didn't die that way. She took her own life shortly after I was born. The family lied to me, blamed my father, said he prevented her career in music, robbed her of her dream. She hanged herself." He stopped, almost holding his breath.

"I'm so sorry," I said, pressing my hand down on his arm. He brushed it away.

"They turned me against my father. I never knew the truth until years later when my father came to Carnegie Hall for my concert. He took me out to dinner and told me the whole story about how my mother had always had mental problems, but the family hushed it up, even from him. He hadn't divorced her. That was another lie. I met his new family, my stepbrother and sister. They were wonderful to me. I couldn't forgive my aunt for what she had done. I never wanted to see her again. Grandma and Grandpa were already gone, but they played their part too. They all did. It was a cruel denial, unforgivable."

I asked him if he ever had contact with his aunt after that. He said he hadn't. I had heard from my mother that after Mr. Loring had died, Mrs. Loring had moved to California to another Spanish hacienda in Santa Barbara where she once again gave piano lessons to children like Harpo and me until one day she suffered a stroke that left her partially paralysed. Harpo wrote to her, and she dictated her replies through her nurse. Mrs. Loring never inquired whether Harpo had any news of Hartley. It was as though a curtain had come down between the two of them. Harpo sent a huge spray of flowers to her funeral when she died. I decided not to tell any of this to Hartley. I was sorry things had turned out so badly for him.

All this happened quite a few years ago now. This past summer, the whole family, along with my mother and Harpo, sailed to Europe on the QE2. I phoned Hartley and Liselotte from New York a month before we sailed and said that we hoped to see them in Zurich again since we had been out of touch for some time. Liselotte said that would be fine, but she warned in a guarded voice that Hartley had been quite ill lately. Then, just three days before we sailed, I received another call from her. She said Hartley was desperately ill now and had had to cancel his concert tour and that it would not be possible for us to see him after all. In fact, she said it would be wiser if we did not call her or even try to see her when we arrived in Zurich because it would only disturb Hartley. She did not say exactly what the illness was, but her voice made it clear that it would be fatal.

We considered canceling the Zurich part of our trip. What would it be without seeing them again? But something seemed to draw me there, and, besides, reservations had been made, and it seemed better to go through with it. My mother and Harpo, both of whom had been fond of Hartley, were naturally curious about where he lived.

There are boats that go out into Lake Zurich and stop at little villages all along its shoreline. In one of those towns lived Liselotte and Hartley. Our boat glided out into the sapphire-blue lake one cold, windy day, with very few people on board. An odd assortment of images: In the middle of the lake a great St. Bernard dog swam strongly to a distant shore; on a grassy slope a large group of nude male bathers gazed at us calmly as our boat provocatively passed close to their beach; a posh-looking garden party in progress under a canopy on an emerald lawn, ladies' dresses and scarves billowing up like pastel clouds in the high wind; an old chateau festooned with hanging baskets of geraniums. And then, suddenly, the grassy headland of the town in which Liselotte and Hartley lived. I pointed it out in silence to my mother and Harpo, letting my hand trail in the water from the side of the boat. There might have been an undercurrent. I don't know, but I felt something rippling against the side of my hand, intimations of something almost forgotten.

Back in New York, after a frustrating day at the old law factory, the taxi dropped me off at my apartment. The jackhammers were still cracking it out on the East River Drive. The 59th Street Bridge loomed up like the skeletal substructure of some constructivist's idea of a city. The flapping slap of traffic over the bridge to Queens clickety-clacked in my ears. A tugboat hooted rudely out on the water. Jerry, the doorman, nodded to me and swung open the door. I rode up in his brass-and-glass elevator. Nobody was home. They were all up in Maine getting the house ready for the summer. I picked up the mail and sorted through it. There was a strange letter, bordered in black, something in German on it. I got out my reading glasses, dropped the New York *Post* along with the rest of the mail, and took a closer look at the letter under a brighter light. I translated it haltingly. "Walter Hartley Skeuse died the 28th day of March. . . Contributions should be made to the Conservatory of Music in Zurich." My body felt heavy and I slumped in a chair. I don't know how long I sat there. Until the tidal wave subsided and I was washed to shore. When I got up, I looked up Rachmaninoff's dates in the encyclopedia. At least he had managed the correct date.

I never made a contribution to the Swiss music school and I never wrote to Liselotte or heard from her again. I don't know why. Sometimes I just freeze up about things and let go. It's so much easier.

But once in a while at night, I find myself waking up, breathing erratically, frightened by something. I have this strange dream of being on board a boat on Lake Zurich, and in this dream we are gliding by a town, and I can distinctly hear music floating down from the headland. My wife and children also hear it. But we can't reach it. The boat sails on with strong, throbbing engines carrying us away, but I am powerless to do anything about our destination. I am so anxious to hold on to the sound of that music that I thrash out my arms toward something I can't really see.

We just keep sailing, sailing until we reach a still point where there is no music, and then in my dream I am propelled into what seems like reality, my old bedroom that I had when I was a boy, where I repeat the things I now do as a man every day: I brush my teeth, shower, go through the city's dirt to my office, into meetings, performing my silent pantomime, smiling at plastic people who smile at me and mouth the words "no problem" and "have a nice day," but I'm left with a gnawing feeling that Chopin, Liszt, and Rachmaninoff have all fled and hidden their hearts away somewhere and I am the only person who knows this, left alone and bereft in my room, unable to explain to people that nobody will ever hear their music again or enter enchanted Spanish haciendas because they no longer exist.

When I wake up, I find to my horror that I am right. Haciendas are only to be found among the broken bones of plastic theme parks and golden arches that line the shore and there is no music anymore, only the recorded sounds of laser-sharp electronic squeals from millions of mutant insects copulating and flying into lights.

PENUMBRA

"Here, kitty, kitty, kitty. Here, kitty, kitty, kitty," called Claude, parting the lower branches of the huge umbrella-like rhododendron so that he could see into its mysteriously dark interior. "I know you are in there. Come on out."

From the blue-blackness, two glass marbles stared out at him, jewels in their natural cave. From up above, he heard the sound of a window being opened. A voice pressed down on him: "Claude, leave the kitty alone. Don't tease her. I am afraid she might claw you."

He drew back quickly from the bush. "All right, grandma. I wasn't going to hurt her."

"I know that. Come on into the sun parlor. Did you bring your things with you?"

"I think so."

"Good. Don't dawdle now. Be a good boy. Leave Perdita alone."

"Yes, grandma," the small boy said, sidling reluctantly up to the sun parlor's garden entrance. Gee whiz, he thought, why did I have to come here? She'll only make me brush my teeth again. She'll push back my cuticles to see if the moons are showing.

The sun parlor intrigued him, though. It was like a mini-Amazon with five green-and-gold cages suspended from the ceiling. There were singing canaries in them, and one a white bird. There was, also, a wonderful fish tank that you could look into and see underwater ballets. And, sometimes, King, the great orange chow, would come into the parlor and sit imperiously like a lion ruling his forest preserve. Only you couldn't touch King at all. "You may look at King, but you must never touch him," cautioned his grandmother. "He doesn't like children." Why not? thought Claude. Why in this polite, well-ordered world of his grandmother should there be the hint of so much violence just under the surface?

Evelyn Turner Bliss looked into the mirror over her dresser trying to see beyond the reflection of her violet eyes, trying to make sense of who she was, where she was, and why she was there. She was sixty-two with black wavy hair and an alabaster complexion, but so serious-looking now, so sour and troubled, when it was still quite clear--she could see it in the mirror--that she had been a Virginia beauty in her youth who had turned many a man's head, notably that of the red-haired Ansel Bliss, an engineer, considered one of Picardy, Virginia's most dynamic citizens. She had married him, lived in Washington, D.C. and Falls Church, until Ansel's retirement when they returned to Picardy and restored the family house in town. Inside a year, though, Ansel was gone, dead of a heart attack, and Evelyn found herself a sudden widow at fifty, with an only son, James, who had married a West Indian woman and had a son, Claude.

On the surface, Evelyn had approved of the marriage. What else could she have done? She lived her life as circumspectly as possible, her presence in town affairs always a deterrant to any unpleasant observations or comments, although there weren't many, the Blisses being regarded as highly intellectual and eccentric, anyway. Her interests, however, narrowed more each year, until they included just gardening (which she did with the aid of Vincent D'Errico) and the one day a week she put in at the Picardy Community Hospital.

Partly because he was alarmed at how much his mother's world was closing in, James, who was a lawyer, moved back from Long Island with his wife, Phyllis, and Claude. Phyllis found life in the small town suffocating, especially the emphasis on church and the genteel roles that many Virginia women were still willing to play. Phyllis, after all, had grown up in the New York metropolitan world. She was used to the play of ideas, the healthy cauldron of cultures. A polite Anglophilia was not for her. James tried to make it easy for her by making many trips up to New York and Washington, but Phyllis felt more hemmed in than ever each time she came back. Her mother-in-law was no help, either, because she, like James, belonged to that secure Virginia world of traditional values, and, if people responded to Phyllis positively, as many did, she felt it was only because she was regarded as some kind of Jamaican exotic. She was aware, too, of the pity she saw in people's eyes when they looked at Claude, her handsome small son with his beautiful milk-chocolate skin, and, worse, she felt Claude must have noticed it too, although he never once asked her about it. She didn't know if he had ever discussed it with James. This, too, bothered her--the thought that her husband as well as her mother-in-law might very well be her enemy. She worried herself into such a neurotic state that her physician had to prescribe tranquillizers which, one day, she took just enough of to send her into a coma from which she never recovered, leaving James, and Claude both with a sense of having been cut off ruthlessly from someone they loved.

Now, as Evelyn examined her reflection in the mirror, she heard her ten-year old grandson clearing his throat downstairs to indicate that he had come into the sun parlor as directed. She picked up her wide-brimmed straw gardening hat, smoothed down her lavender dress and glided noiselessly down the stairs. Claude saw her silhouetted in the entrance, a dark figure moving into a world of ferns against sunlight. She swooped down gracefully to his level and offered her cheek for a kiss.

Claude pulled away, as she was afraid he might do.

She decided to treat it lightly. "What's the matter, Claude? Is Grandmother so old, so unpleasant that you don't want to kiss her?"

"No."

"What is it, then?"

"It's just that sometimes ladies have dry powder on their faces. I hate it. It gets up my nose and makes me sneeze."

Impulsively, she pulled him to her and kissed him fiercely. He rolled his eyes. "Oh, don't be foolish," she said. "That's just a face we women put on 'to prepare a face to meet the faces that we meet,' as Mr. T. S. Eliot says. That's just a dusty rose." She thought to win him over through diversion now. She would show him the riches of her Henri Rousseau world.

"Come over here. I have some surprises for you. But, goodness, what's this? There's mud on your shoes. Did you wipe your feet before you came in?"

"I thought I did."

"Thought you did? But, dear, you must be more thorough. You have to be careful with that Virgina red earth. You have to scrape it off. Now, here, use that cocoa mat right there. That's better."

She looked at his face to gauge his reaction. "What's that you're chewing? Is that gum?"

Claude threw his hands over his mouth as though the interior had a sinful mind of its own. "Yes, grandma."

She held out her palm. "Here, spit it into my hand."

He did, and she threw the hated substance in the wastebasket. Claude heard her murmur something about lack of manners and how Mr.Wrigley had ruined the country, but, he thought, what can you expect from a grandmother anyway?

She pointed him toward the aquarium. "Look at that angel fish. Do you see it swimming?"

"Yes."

"Do you know what it does if someone touches the glass in front of it?"

"No."

"It blushes."

"Blushes? That's crazy. Fish can't blush."

"Yes, they can. Try it and see."

He put his hand up against the pane of glass separating him from the lacquered world. He watched. The stripes on the fish actually became lighter. "Why does it do that?" he asked.

"Because it doesn't really want people to notice it. It's a defense trick. I call that fish *La Grande Coquette.*"

"Why?"

"That means it flirts with us all, teases us."

"It's funny that it does that, all right."

"Look here in this cage. Did you see my new bird?"

"That white one?"

"Yes. She's called *Amarantha.* That's Latin for "unfading, undying." I hope it's true. I want this bird to live on forever. Have you heard her sing yet?"

"No. Does she?"

"Oh, yes. She's a chopper. Like a nightingale. Sometimes she will sing in the middle of the night. You might wake up this evening and hear her. I heard her the other night, well, really, morning, about five o'clock, I think it was."

"She is beautiful. I wish I could pat King."

"No, no, no, Claude. He's an old boy. He's a grump. We mustn't touch him. He doesn't understand affection."

"What good is a dog like that?"

"Well, he was a puppy once, young and frisky, but he's forgotten that. I don't think he really likes or understands birds. He doesn't appreciate the sounds they make. I think they hurt his ears. Dogs have supersensitive hearing sometimes."

"I brought my things," Claude said abruptly, indicating a flimsy blue laundry box into which he had rolled up all his choice worldly treasures.

Evelyn picked up the box. "What do you have in here?"

"I brought my butterfly collection. Be careful. Hold it flat."

"You did?"

"Yes. I caught another tiger swallow-tail yesterday. Can I go out into the garden, grandma?"

"Of course. But, first, let's get you settled. I'm putting you in the back bedroom. You can see the whole garden from there. There are all the butterflies in the world a boy could want, and birds and trees--but, remember, you can only climb in the apple and cherry trees. The others are too dangerous."

"I'm only going to stay here tonight."

"I thought your father said two nights."

"He said he'll call tomorrow morning. I may go home then."

"Well, come on. Let's go up the wooden hill to your room and get you settled.

Claude heard the sound of someone whistling in the distance. He looked out the window and saw Vincent, the gardener, standing there in his white undershirt and baggy pants, muscular brown arms and strong hands cupped to his lips now to project his tune. Vincent looked up to the second storey and saw Claude peering out at him from behind the screen. "Hello, Claude. What are you doing here?"

Claude opened the screen, looked out, focusing on Vincent's light blue eyes full of hidden laughter. "Hunting butterflies. Will I be in your way?" Claude flashed his butterfly net at Vincent.

"No. Watch out for the peonies, though. And those dahlias. They are your grandmother's favorites."

"I'm coming down." Claude slipped down the back stairs to the garden. Vincent looked bigger to him now. "I don't like peonies, anyway," he said. "Neither do butterflies. Peonies get those little red ants all over them. I don't see why you bother with them."

"I am paid to bother with them." Vincent felt he had to say something more to the boy. "Claude?"

"Yes, Vincent?"

"I was sorry to hear about your mother."

"Yes. Thank you." Claude deliberately picked up the crown sprinkler on the end of the garden hose and dumped it down in a different place. "Do you know what, Vincent?" he said.

"What?"

"There are moths. They come out at night and they are much more beautiful than butterflies."

"I've heard about them."

"There is one called Polyphemus. It has eyes all over it like a peacock."

"Peacock's eyes?"

"Yes. And there is one called the Luna moth. It is light green and dances in the sky at night like a ballet dancer when no one is looking. And do you know what else, Vincent?

"What?"

"You catch moths by putting out beer at night."

"You're kidding."

"No. They really like it. And there's more. Did you know that moths were a symbol of immortality to the Egyptians?"

"Immortality? Egyptians? Well, I never heard that one."

"Yes. They really believed it. Do you know what immortality is? Vincent, do you know or not?"

"No. Tell me what it is."

"It means that when you die you don't really die, but you live forever."

"How can that be?"

"You live in someone's memory and you are never forgotten. I know it's true because my father told me so and I have a strong memory."

"Well, he is right, son."

"My mother never really left me, you see. I don't have to feel sad if I don't want to."

"I understand. It's like my wife will always be close to me too. I always still feel her there when I go home at night. Now, come over here, son. Give me a hand with this hose. You put it in the wrong place. I see your grandmother looking out at us."

Claude's father, James Bliss, opened up the iron gate that led into the driveway and drove his car in, stopping just inside. He got out, carefully closing and locking the gate behind him. He crossed the front lawn to the garden at the side and back of the house. Leading into the garden was a statue of a young boy, more of an Hippolytus than an Eros. It faced toward the center of the garden which was laid out in an *etoile* pattern. He looked around. All paths led to the center, he remembered, but there was no boy there now. Just him.

"Jamie?" A hopeful voice called from the front door.

"Yes, mother?"

"I heard you drive up. Come around to the front."

"Just a minute. I was looking for Claude. I'd forgotten how peaceful it is here." The only sound he heard was the passionate whistling of the gardener who had launched into *"Di Provenza il mar il suol"* from *La Traviata*. James smiled. He felt happy and secure because this was the known world to which he belonged.

Claude lay upside down in the heart of the dark green rhododendron, having routed the great jungle cat, Perdita, who slithered around the side of the house, plotting her revenge. Claude lay suspended as he squinted through the twisted branches of the large nest-like shrub. He was entranced by the great swatches of sunlight and shadow dramatically cutting across the yard, hinting of mysterious clouds above. He heard the low, summery sound of thunder cracking ominously in the distance. He heard the lazy, familiar voices of his father and grandmother. He heard the nervous chirping of the canary birds in their green-and-gold cages sensing something--the approaching storm? The stalking cat? The menace in the rhododendron?

He thought about his mother. He remembered how unhappy she was whenever she visited this house he was at, how his grandmother was always questioning him about what his mother was planning or doing at their home, as though she could never do anything right. He remembered the tensions that riffled up in little flashes between his mother and father whenever his grandmother called on the phone or gave Claude or his father presents at Christmas and on their birthdays. He knew that his grandmother never really liked his mother and, because of that, he knew he could never really like his grandmother. He supposed she was glad now that his mother had died.

Claude shifted position, right side up now, and looked into the glassed-in conservatory of the great grandmother jungle. What if he made a foray into this Amazon world to see for himself the great white singing bird up close? What if he broke all rules and stole a treasured possession?

He pulled over a chair to a spot directly underneath the cage. He climbed up on the chair, peered into the cage, watching avariciously every little movement of the bird. He cupped the birdcage in one hand, opened the little door with the other, and tried to coax the bird toward the opening. The bird jumped on its perch and ruffled its feathers. Claude, still holding the cage, suddenly lost his balance, unhooked the cage by mistake, and fell over with the cage still clutched in his arms. Impulsively, he sat up, held up the cage to see if the bird was all right. He opened the little door quickly and whispered: "Fly, Amarantha. Fly away, bird." Then he opened the screen door to the larger world so that the frightened bird flew out into the garden.

Claude's father and grandmother came around the side of the house and saw Claude sprawled on the floor of the sun parlor. "Claude," cried out Evelyn. "What is it? What have you done?" She saw the empty cage in his lap. "You've let Amarantha out."

"I just wanted to see her up close," Claude said. "The birdcage fell." He looked away.

His father, still outside, plucked something pulsating like a beating heart off the rhododendron. "Here it is, Mother," he said. "On the rhododendron."

Claude saw his grandmother shoot her hand inside his father's hands to receive and cradle the frightened bird. She stroked it, holding it securely in her tight right hand. "There, there," she said. "Poor baby. You're safe. Into your home now." She plunged it back into its cage which James had handed her and then she stood on the footstool and hooked the cage back up to the ceiling.

"Why did you do this, Claude?" asked his father.

"What was in your mind?" said his grandmother pinching him sharply on his upper arm.

"I didn't mean anything. I just wanted to see something, I guess." He drew away from both of them now, but he didn't cry. He wondered what would happen next. He saw himself as a small boy who came into a garden once and learned that God was a woman who so loved her world that she was unwilling to give up her only begotten son and grandson, only the woman and the memory of the woman who had taken them both away from her. But Claude was determined not to let it happen. He caught a glimpse of Vincent watching the scene as he shifted the hose. He thought he saw Vincent's head move slightly up and down.

The wind rose suddenly now and the thunder grew closer.

His father said quietly: "Claude, get your things. We're going home now."

Claude said nothing but walked past his grandmother to get his laundry box, not daring to look at her, knowing that her eyes would be deeply troubled pools of unhappiness now because he had won, at least for the time being.

WHEN HERMES PAN RULED THE WORLD

1938: A sunny Friday in May. I am in my room in the middle of the Camaroons somewhere, pasting up stamps into my Scott's Stamp Album. I vaguely hear Terrie's voice calling me through the jungle. "Skip, it's quarter to five. You need to get the victrola ready."

"What?"

"It's quarter to five. Toots will be here by six. You know that."

Terrie appeared, looking irritated, in the doorway of my room.

I came to, flew out of the Camaroons on instant recall, and landed back into reality. "Yes," I said. "I know. The victrola is down in the basement."

"Well, get it then," said Terrie.

"You get it," I said. "I've got to finish with my stamps."

"I'm going to dance "Who's Your Little Whoosis?" Terrie said, swirling around. "I wonder what Toots will bring today?"

"Did you ever hear of a song called "Dardanella? "I asked.

"No," Terrie replied.

"I heard it on the radio today. I liked it."

"Toots will know it, if anybody will,"Terrie said. "I'd give anything to have one of those feathery outfits like the one Ginger Rogers wore in *Top Hat.*"

"Heaven, I'm in Heaven," I sang. Terrie swayed in the doorway, turning around, showing her back, and pursing her lips as though she were Ginger Rogers dancing away.

Each Friday, Toots would come home bearing Decca records for us to try on the victrola. I think she paid something like $1.00 for three hit records. She would buy them somewhere in the deepest recesses of Brooklyn after she finished her work at the Williamsburgh Savings Bank. She told us that building was the tallest one in Brooklyn, just as the Empire State Building was the tallest one in Manhattan and only a few years old. Toots was a source of endless interest to Terrie and me. She didn't just work. She called it "going to business." She was our mother's youngest sister, had been a flapper in the 1920s, was dumped out onto the job market in the depression, and had been engaged for over seven years to a nice young man named Jimmy who was doomed to die of tuberculosis.

Toots' real name was Angelina. She was tall and attractive, looked very much like Loretta Young, the movie actress, who was approximately her same age. In fact, Toots had gone to P.S. 152 in Brooklyn with Barbara Stanwyck, who was then called Ruby Stevens. Ruby wrote in Toots' autograph book, "Remember the future, remember the past. Remember the fun we had in Miss Hagen's class." Toots told us that Ruby Stevens was a good dancer at age fourteen, that she went into Broadway shows and then to the movies where she became the very glamorous actress. Toots, too, had hoped to dance, but she never did anything about it. She said that should be a lesson to Terrie and me--that if we wanted fame, we'd better get started dancing. To help us and to keep the old spark alive in herself, she would bring home records every Friday, and she, Terrie and I would dance around the living room to the sounds of "I'm Putting All My Eggs in One Basket" as though we were all flying Fred Astaires and Ginger Rogers. Toots would take us to see all their movies and then we would zap around at home for days after singing "A Fine Romance," and "I Won't Dance, Don't Ask Me." Toots also modeled the dresses she bought--she called them "numbers" or "creations" for her business in the bank. "Here's a little number I bought at Ohrbach's," she would say. Or "This little creation I picked up at the Madam's." We later learned that was her euphemistic name for S. Klein's on Fourteenth Street.

Toots lived with us during most of the 1930s in our house in East Rockaway on Long Island, about twenty-three miles from the City. Toots commuted on the Long Island Railroad, and she would walk the twenty-minute distance from the railroad station to our house. Terrie and I used to appear out on the street in front of the house and look down the long road through the huge oak trees to see if we spotted her far away. Half the neighborhood would watch with us, too. Nobody was more eagerly welcomed by the youngsters than was Toots. She liked kids and was the essence of glamor to us all. Shortly after her arrival, the sounds of music issuing from our little black portable victrola that you had to crank up before it would go could be heard wafting from our house. We supplied the Hit Parade to the entire neighborhood. When dinner was ready, Toots, who would help Mother in the kitchen, would say, "'Soup's on, kiddies,'" and off we would fly to the table where we sat opposite Toots, watching her attentively because she had the unusual ability to inhale smoke from a cigarette, eat a mouthful of food, and then out would come smoke again. She and my father smoked, even during meals. My mother, Terrie, and I didn't, although once or twice Terrie and I had tried to do the Toots' trick on the sly. It didn't work. I was only ten and Terrie twelve. It was just a bad first try, I guess.

Toots had lived with my grandfather in his creepy wooden house in Brooklyn until he died and the house was sold. Our house was fairly large, so she came to live with us. She slept in the bedroom over the garage which she called the icebox because, somehow, the steam heat in the house never really reached there, although it sure made sizzling noises, groans, and great cracking noises in the rest of the house.

In our house, my father and Toots were the clowns, always laughing, always finding things hilariously funny. My mother was the serious one, getting Terrie and me off to school, paying the bills, seeing that the house was cleaned, saying no to the Fuller brushman and other door-to-door salespeople who would knock on the front door, bringing danger and adventure whenever they were permitted to demonstrate their products.

The thing we most looked forward to in 1938, aside from the next Fred and Ginger movie was the New York World's Fair of 1939. We would sometimes persuade my father to get out the 1936 grey Buick and drive along Grand Central Parkway to see how everything was coming along. We could hardly wait to move into the World of the Future. I began keeping a scrapbook about it. 1939 would be something to live for. The World of Tomorrow would be streamlined, clean, beautiful, with chromium and certitude for all.

Toots proved to me, at least, that the movies in the 1930s were not mere escapist dramas. Life was exactly like them. Toots was the quintessential heroine. Her whole life was a '30s movie. If Barbara Stanwyck had to give up a daughter named Laurel only to be told to move on by a policeman in *Stella Dallas*, so Toots had her sad love affair with the hospitalized Jimmy. If Katharine Hepburn, as Susan, had her madcap adventure with paleontologist Cary Grant in *Bringing Up Baby*, so Toots had similar looney adventures in real life, once when a St. Bernard attached itself to her and followed her home from the station during a snowstorm, refusing to budge from her side, and actually living with us for two weeks until Mother said "enough is enough" and called the Bide-a-Wee Home to come rescue the monster. For Christmas once, I had desperately wanted a collie dog, after reading Albert Payson Terhune's many books on all the collies in his life. My mother, of course, said no, but Toots gave me a canary bird (acceptable to my mother) which I promptly called "Lad," in honor of one of Terhune's most celebrated dogs. Toots played along with me and treated Lad as though he were a dog, too. Believing was everything.

Terrie and I loved the way Toots regarded herself, not as though she were a human being, but as though she were a department store, like Macy's. "Well, how's the Hair Department?" she would ask, looking in the mirror to check

her hair-do. Or "the Face Department," which meant
mascara, eyebrow pencil, powder, rouge, and lipstick. "The
Hands Department" meant shiny red nail polish. The "Shoe
Department" meant those high heels Toots wore to do the
choreography required at the Williamsburgh Savings Bank.
And so on. Her department store was something to be
rebuilt every morning and then checked out carefully before
going off to present itself to the working world. Terrie and I
were enlisted as impartial critics. My mother, of course,
thought Toots was frivolous. I think she felt the three of us
were slightly nuts. She had serious work to do around the
house. When she was mad at me she would sometimes say
she thought I had a screw loose. But we all managed
somehow. We were happy and thriving then. My father
earned around $50 a week as a copywriter for a Manhattan
sports magazine. Toots earned $18 a week, and Terrie and I
sometimes took bottles back to the A & P or Piggly Wiggly
and got 25 cents for the lot of them.

Sometimes in art galleries these days, I catch glimpses of
paintings by Reginald Marsh, Edward Hopper, or Charles
Burchfield and I think I see Toots there, although I'm always
wrong. It's just the idea of her. But the other day, opening up
some old cartons in the attic, out fell a yellowed clipping
from the Brooklyn *Eagle* which showed Toots in a bathing
suit sitting on the beach at Ocean Beach, Fire Island. The
caption underneath read "Cheering the Sad Sea Waves is Miss
Toots Spanos of Brooklyn."And there she is, smiling her
Loretta Young Smile for all the world to enjoy. I remember
Ocean Beach. We rented a bungalow there for five years in
the summers from 1934 to 1938.

I've often felt bad that the depression didn't bite us as
badly as it did other people. Maybe it was because
everybody in our house voted for Franklin Roosevelt so we
thought things were going along just fine, improving all the
time. We weren't typical, though. Most of our neighbors
were hard-line Nassau County Republicans. Toots told Terrie
and me not to be afraid of people high-hatting us because we

were Democrats but just to go on concentrating for our futures."Potatoes are cheaper, tomatoes are cheaper," Toots would sing, "Now's the time to fall in love." We agreed. We wanted more than anything for her to marry Jimmy and live happily ever after.

Jimmy was really nice. He used to come by in his Chevy coupe with its magical rumble seat, pile Terrie and me into the back, Toots in the front, and zoom on down to Long Beach or Point Lookout at the heady speed of 25 miles per hour. I remember once we got a ticket, passing through Lido Beach. We thought the policeman was mean, giving such a thoughtful person as Jimmy a ticket. Jimmy was tall and handsome, looked like Gary Cooper to us. The only problem, my mother said, was that Jimmy was a Protestant. We were Catholic. My mother said it was hard for a Catholic to marry a Protestant. Terrie and I couldn't see why. Jimmy was the perfect man. He loved kids and he loved Toots.

But he had these running attacks of tuberculosis and had to be hospitalized from time to time. This last time, he had been in for quite a few months. Some Fridays, Toots didn't come home on time. Instead, she went to the hospital to see Jimmy, had dinner with him, and then came home on a later train, when it was dark. Occasionally she had been crying. We could see that. She would hold muffled conversations with mother in another room. My father would often be in on those secret meetings. Terrie and I wondered what all the fuss was about. Why was Toots unhappy? Why was she not telling Terrie and me all about it? We already knew that there might be some sadness in happy endings, that everything wasn't perfect. The game could still go on, couldn't it?

One day my father brought home from his office a young man who worked with him as a sports writer. This man's name was Zan, short for Alexander. He lived in Garden City with his parents and five sisters. My father had told us that Zan was a snappy dresser, buying his clothes at Rogers Peet, and that he liked golf and was a New York Giants fan.

Toots cooked the dinner the night Zan appeared. My father and Toots went into gales of laughter over this meal, which was pork and beans, because Toots had not soaked the beans the night before and so they were as hard as hailstones when they came to the table. My father picked them up and shot them off his knuckles like marbles all over the walls and ceiling in the dining room. My mother was not amused, but Toots and Father howled with laughter, taking Terrie and me along with them, and finally even Mother and Zan broke down and laughed. After dinner, Father pushed Terrie and me into the kitchen to help Mother while he and Zan talked with Toots in the living room. We liked Zan, even though Mother prophesied he would never set foot inside our asylum again. During dinner, Zan had praised our father at work and talked about other writers and journalists he liked. We thought business must be fun to go to because everyone seemed to be having such a great time.

While we were drying dishes in the kitchen, Toots called out, "Skipper, where's that victrola?" I told her it was up in my room and I heard her go upstairs, and then come down again, and eventually I heard the sounds of "That Old Feeling" coming from the living room. I could tell she was in a good mood because she called me "Skipper." That always meant full speed ahead.

When we finished the dishes, which was much sooner than usual, I looked into the living room, and Zan was dancing with Toots very close, cheek to cheek. He even gave a little nuzzle right into her neck. Terrie shot me one of her most significant looks. There was Toots dancing right into another starring role as produced by Pandro S. Berman and directed by Mark Sandrich with Fred and Ginger choreography by Hermes Pan. It had to be true, Terrie swore. She claimed Hermes Pan was the only Greek god she'd ever worship.

Funny how the sadness in Toots' life brought on by Jimmy's illness quickly swept into the exhilaration brought on by the advent of Zan. For Toots' birthday, he gifted her with a large amethyst ring, convincing Terrie and me, at least, that this was no ordinary birthday present. Fridays were now put on suspension in our house, although occasionally Toots and Zan would surprise us, coming home from the city with the records we loved so much--Ella Fitzgerald and Chick Webb, Bing Crosby, Jimmy Lunceford and his Orchestra. We geared ourselves up for the Big Wedding which we knew was coming, although our mother said not to be so serious, she knew nothing about it. But you could tell from Toots' eyes how happy she was. "Well, the Face Department looks pretty good," she would say. "How's the Hat Department? We're stepping out tonight." The Astor, the Roosevelt, the Biltmore, the Waldorf-Astoria, the Stork Club, Ethel Merman in *Panama Hattie*--We had to hear about each exciting evening on the town.

One Friday, though, Toots came home late. Our mother met her and rushed her right up to her room, away from Terrie and me, with no explanation. We didn't realize at first what was going on, but Terrie soon figured it out and clued me in on it. Toots had had to tell Jimmy that she couldn't marry him but was going to marry Zan instead. Terrie acted it all out for me, so that I burst into tears, causing the two of us to sit there for a moment hugging each other with the desperation and pain of it all. How could Toots go on? How could we go on? It was like that terrible moment in *The Old Maid* when Bette Davis' mean daughter told her what did she know about love, she was nothing but an old maid. Buckets!

Over the weekend Toots stayed pretty much in her room, until Sunday afternoon when Zan came over to take her out for a drive. She came down the stairs looking very pale and thin and asked us did we mind if we didn't go on the drive with them today. We said no, of course, we didn't, and I know she could tell from our extreme politeness that we knew, understood, and sympathized with her. When she came back from the drive, she was *Theodora Goes Wild* again.

The wedding was the big thing now. Terrie and I wanted an MGM extravaganza, a Norma Shearer fantasy, produced by Irving S. Thalberg. We saw yards and yards of tulle for the wedding gown. We wanted acres of flowers and our mother done up in a Garbo-John Frederic's chapeau. Jennie expected to be the flower girl and I the ring bearer. The music would be Wagner out of Max Steiner. Our father would be debonair, like Cary Grant. The priest would be Spencer Tracy. The reception would be *Flying Down to Rio* with dancing girls on one hundred grand pianos, all choreographed by Busby Berkeley.

That was our fantasy, and that was all wrong. The wedding, it turned out, was a big problem. Toots was Catholic and Zan was Methodist. The priest apparently was Father Monkey Wrench. Mother broke the bad news to Terrie and me. The wedding would take place in an underground chapel at St. Anthony's Church in Oceanside. Only fifteen people could fit inside. Terrie and I were not to be among them. We were crushed. We had saved up our money to buy Zan and Toots a very large blue vase capable of holding enormous dahlias or giant chrysanthemums, and now we were to be denied the pleasure of watching our favorite person on earth reach the happy ending we so much wanted for her. But we made the best of it. We were on the front lawn smiling and waving when Toots left for the church and we were there waiting when our father and mother came home hours later to tell us all about it and to report how Zan and Toots looked when they left in his Chevy for Williamsburg, Virginia. Mother said they looked harried and that Zan had drunk too much champagne. Father, who was the Best Man, said the priest forgot Zan's name in the middle of the ceremony and asked him what it was, but Father said the wedding was just fine, that everything went off as planned. Terrie and I took a long time to get over our extreme disappointment.

When the honeymoon was over, Zan and Toots moved into the Phipps Garden Apartments in Springfield Gardens. I remember visiting them there because they were the first people in our family to live in a real apartment. I recall that it was brick, resembling Hampton Court in England, that it had nice green spaces and shrubs in an interior courtyard and that out of Toots' window I heard music playing, looked out and saw that there was an organ grinder and his monkey down there. Toots, Terrie, and I ran down to watch this man with his whimsical monkey who reached out his little hand to take pennies from you and then tipped his cap with his hand in thanks.

The World's Fair had now begun in Flushing Meadows and we made several trips to it with our family and Zan and Toots. If Toots' wedding had been a one-star motion picture for us, the World's Fair was a four-star event, proof that life could imitate art, if it tried hard enough. General Motors provided the whole overview with its panorama of the World of the Future which one rode into, seated on an upholstered couch no less. Puppets sang and danced in *La Traviata* at the House of Jewels. Ford cars bounced down the Ford ramp in lacquered reds, blues, and yellows. Fountains danced in pulsating colors in the Lagoon of Nations. The Russians had a grand pavillion, Italy had another with a waterfall coursing down it, and at the center of the fair the Trylon and Perisphere symbolized the geometry of the future. Terrie and I knew what was coming then. We had seen ourselves in the flickering blue light of early television, we had jumped back from the lightning in the G. E. pavillion. The future would be something that nobody could control. It would be illuminating but extremely dangerous.

However, the immediate future was something that I did control, oddly enough. About a year after the wedding, sometime in the fall of 1940, I was home alone in the afternoon. My mother was out shopping and Terrie was playing the cello with the Nassau County Youth Symphony. I remember that it was a scrappy, windy October day, with the brown leaves from the tall oak trees swirling furiously by the casement windows of our house, startling me because they were ghostly bat-like intruders into the periphery of my studying. I was so engrossed in my geography—sailing down the Amazon toward the great rain forest of Brazil—that at first I didn't notice the urgent knocking at the front door. The bell didn't work and people always had to pound double-hard on our solid oak door to be heard. Suddenly, I was aware of the insistent knock, went to the door, opened it, and there was Jimmy, looking really healthy, with an attractive, nervous young woman smiling next to him. "Skip," he said, offering his hand. "How are you?"

"Jimmy," I said. "What are you doing here?"

"Just stopped by on my way into the city from Wading River. Wanted to show off my bride. Anne, this is Skip. Skip, Anne is my wife."

"Well, what do you know," I gasped. "Pleased to meet you." She shook my hand. I held on a little too long. I didn't know what to say.

"May we come in?" said Jimmy.

"Sure." I pointed toward the living room and closed the door.

"Is your mother home? Jimmy asked.

"No, she's out shopping. Gosh, I can't believe you're married, Jimmy."

Jimmy looked at Anne and held her hand. "Two months ago," he said. "How's your mother? Your dad?"

"Just fine"

"Everybody?"

"Just fine." I froze. I was no good at adult talk.

"How old must you be now?" Jimmy asked me.

"Twelve," I said.

"We used to go to the beach," Jimmy explained to Anne. "The whole family."

"It's so rough," said Anne, "the ocean."

"Anne's family has a place at Candlewood Lake in Connecticut," said Jimmy. "She's a lake and mountain woman. We live in Scarsdale now."

"Oh," I said. "Would you like a root beer, ginger ale, or something?"

. "No, thanks," Jimmy said, getting up. "We have to be getting on. Just give my best to your family."

At the door I blurted out. "You look wonderful, Jimmy. Thanks for stopping by."

Jimmy put his arm around my shoulder and kind of hugged me. Then he and Anne walked to their car, not a little flivver anymore, but something with four doors--a Studebaker, I think it was. Then they were gone. I was flabbergasted.

I never told anyone that Jimmy had stopped by. I had seen enough tear-jerking movies to know this news might break everyone's heart. I didn't want Toots to be hurt, ever. She had thought Jimmy would probably never come out of the hospital, that he would die of tuberculosis. We all thought so, too. But here he was in his own happy ending, just the same way Toots was in hers. I thought it was too tragic to believe, these two ships that passed each other in the night and missed. How would Toots feel knowing she had dismissed the real love of her life only to have him saved by another? This was the adult world of complex high emotions that I was being initiated into. I wasn't sure whether I could get through life like this. Why couldn't everything be charted and certain, as in my schoolbooks? I felt then that I was doomed to fall in love with some gorgeous heroine and be discarded by mistake, the same way Toots had cast off Jimmy. I would have to be on my guard as I marched into the World of the Future.

I didn't know then that Sunday, December 7, 1941 was just around the corner. I didn't know then that Jimmy would be dead of tuberculosis within two years. I didn't know then that Toots and Zan would move far away to Houston, Texas, and that I would only see them on rare occasions. What I remember most is that sharp stab in my stomach as I waited for something magical to happen, for the music to begin.

DORIS

The problem is I never knew who Doris was. I have often wondered about her, visualized her, even thought I'd seen her in crowds--you know, around Christmastime, darting into Bonwit Teller's or rounding the corner of the Public Library on Copley Square, but I never had any proof it was really she--just a hint of her, actually, an infuriating subliminal suggestion of somebody who insinuated herself into my life one day because of a stupid telephone call, leaving me to wonder what it was all about and why I had to be the wrong number on that particular day.

I was minding my own business that morning, finishing up a canvas in the brilliant new abstract expressionist style I was ploughing through. You know, laying the paint on heavily with the palette knife in that thick impasto technique, heavy with bold strokes and willful distortions, reflecting a view of Boston that I thought was revolutionary, but really was idiotic, because Boston isn't like that, never was, and never will be, so far as I can tell. But what did I know? I was twenty-five then, desperate for some kind of attention in the art world, in which, so far, I had only succeeded with pale watercolors in the John Marin manner.

A splash of carmine, a squeeze of yellow chrome, and suddenly the telephone rings, just as I am in the middle of a gorgeous swooping downstroke, creating a vermilion vapor trail from outer space. I stop in mid-flight, pick up the phone, and this woman's voice says, "Have you gone into the shower yet?"

"No," I replied.

"Do me a favor," the voice says. "Have you got some paper and a pencil handy."

"No."

"Go, get some before you go into the shower."

"Hang on." I went over to the table where I keep all the paperclips, envelopes, stamps, and pencils, got a little notepad and a stubby pencil, and returned to the phone. "Okay," I said.

"Doris called, and she is terribly upset. I want you to call her. Write this down."

"Doris?" I asked, trying to place her.

"She was in tears. I want you to call 482-1283 and explain everything to her just as soon as I hang up."

"Explain?" Nothing rang a bell.

"482-1283. Do it right now."

"But who is she?"

"Don't play games. Call her," the voice demanded, dropping into the lower register with a terrible urgency, and hung up.

I looked at the notepad. I physically bopped myself on top of my head to see if the name "Doris" meant anything at all. I thought of all the Dorises I had ever known. There was Doris Brown in the first grade at school--a pale, almost albino child who looked maybe one hundred years old, with straight white hair, owlish eye-glasses, and perenially drooping drawers, so that we all sang, "Doris Brown, Doris Brown, went to town, with her britches hanging down," in our cruel, thoughtless way. Then there was Doris Mae Jones from Montgomery, Alabama, who was swift and blonde, blue-eyed and fairly wicked. She was in my sister's class in the eighth grade, and they all went riding on horses after school at the stables out near Thoreau's pond in Concord. One look from that Doris and I took up horseback riding myself until she threw me over for a D. H. Lawrence older man with a mustache who was the riding master and wore jodhpurs, boots, and all that jazz. That was the end of that. The only other Doris I knew was a secretary in a publishing company where I worked briefly after leaving Harvard. This Doris wore no makeup, no deodorant, and sported clothes that looked as though they had first spent twenty-five years on the rack at the Goodwill. She lived in Wollaston with her mother and flaunted her genteel poverty in front of all the flashier types in the office. Everyone hated her.

But none of these Dorises had ever had more than the most passing relationship to my life. There were no currents and crosscurrents. Once in, once out. They were ghosts from the unmemorable past. Who was this new Doris? Was she just a telephonic mistake, not really intended for me at all? Was there some strange mixup between A.T. & T. and M.C.I? Or, did some faintly sinister presence in the universe, some distant god, set her in motion just to trip me up?

From what I know, the woman who called me was well-educated, a nice, modulated voice. I'd say she was about forty, maybe, and calling from Wellesley. I remember thinking "Wellesley" at the time, not "Wayland" or "Newton." There is a difference. "Wellesley"--something learned-suburban and upper-middle about her. Something that suggested a dean or a woman of some importance. Naturally, I immediately assumed that Doris had to be my age--twenty-five, or maybe a little younger. I could actually see Doris with her high forehead, her clear-blue, intelligent eyes focused on something, one hand brushing back the bangs of her blondish hair, staring with intensity at something. What? Do you think she could see me? Could she picture me at the telephone, nervously biting the eraser on the pencil in concern over her plight, while the dean or her mother in Wellesley phoned to tell me that Doris was in trouble?

"482-1283." The number leaped out at me. "Call it," I said aloud. "Not yet," said the artist in me. "Finish that downstroke first. Get that great comet's tail into your painting." So I did, defining, directing, bringing that huge sucker of vermilion into a perfect landing. Then I picked up the telephone and dialed 482-1283, my normally steady hand with an odd little tremor in it now.

The other end buzzed once. I was poised expectantly, but then an irritating tink-tank-tonk sound came on, followed by a mechanical recorded voice saying, "We're sorry. You have reached a number that is disconnected or is no longer in service." Thinking I had dialed incorrectly, I checked out what I had written on the notepad. "482-1283" all right. I dialed again, and the superior voice of the machine repeated its unwanted message. I hung up, feeling frustrated by the unfairness of this obsessive mystery, and went back to my painting which now took on a stormy appearance with dark abstract blobs strangely like distorted telephones looming in the cosmos of this particular canvas.

By noon, curiously, I still couldn't shake the problem. I used my entire lunch hour to race over to Back Bay station where it suddenly occurred to me that I might find a clue to Doris, who I now had determined, was on the point of departure for somewhere. I thought I might find a hint in a phone booth, for instance, perhaps the fragment of a discarded note, or a telephone directory turned to a certain page. I was amazed at the strength of my obsession. But nothing turned up. I scanned the faces of hurrying passengers, but none turned toward me, none gave me any kind of an answer. I gave up, so I thought.

After dinner that night, which I sulked through silently with some friends down in the Quincy Market, I impulsively hailed a taxi and had the cabbie drive me out to Logan Airport on a hunch. The thought hit me that Doris might be on a plane bound for Morocco or Australia, some place very distant from the trouble in her life. I cased the lounges, scrutinized the passengers like a detective, looking for a sign, just the merest suggestion of one. The closest I got was, as a group of passengers bound for London were being taken through the British Airways gate to go out to their waiting plane far out in the field, the doors of the shuttle in which they were being transported closed with jailhouse finality, as a steel curtain slid across their faces. A young woman in the press of people near the door smiled enigmatically at me very quickly, leaving only the image, as the door slammed out her smile and face from me forever. What was she smiling at, I wondered? The tenseness, the anxiety in my face? Was it amusing to her? Was she reassuring me, or what? Did she know something?

The whole situation continued to nag at me long after. After all, I had agreed to be the rescuer. I had done as I was told. There had been an obvious emergency, and I had responded properly. I did not feel ashamed of what I did. "Save Doris" was the main thought on my mind. I wanted to. I was capable. I had been chosen. But the woman had hung up, thinking everything was fine, and then I had hesitated, and so I had not exactly done what I was supposed to when I should have done it, and that has bothered me ever since, even if I did get a disconnected number when I finally acted. I am a completer of assignments. I do not like to leave any tag ends ever.

I now must resort to a public plea. I, of course, cannot advertise in the "Personals" section of certain newspapers because Doris would not read them, nor would I. But there are definite things that must be said here and now.

Doris, whoever you are, wherever you are, I am here. I have gone to the shower now. I am clean and ready. You have only to call me at my home on Joy Street, and I promise I will drop whatever I am doing to come and save you from whatever perilous situation you may be in. I love you, Doris. Call when you want me.

THE BUS ON THE VIA TRIUMPHANS

The reason I am blabbing all this out is it seems I have become the news of the day on the central coast of California. Everybody wants to know what I thought of the great kidnapping--the news reporters, a television lady from Santa Barbara, and somebody even told me that the L.A. *Times* put in a call to the judge. So I'd like to set the record straight as I experienced it, and then get back to a little less excitement in my life, if you don't mind. That albino pseudo-artist who said everybody gets fifteen minutes of fame didn't know beans about the subject. I've had five or six of those moments already, and this was just another one of them. I take them in my stride. They're common as earthquakes in California.

Anyway, here's how I saw it. Every morning at exactly 8:26 I board the bus at the corner of the Via Triumphans and Field for the trip into Rivas de la Luna where I work in the Halfway House from 9 to 5, packing lunches made by the kitchen staff for people who need them.

I perform my job mostly in silence, as I have for the last ten years. I found, as I grew older, that people listened less and cared less about what I had to say. So I just stopped talking about important things one day, and it's all worked out just fine ever since. I say "Good morning" and "Have a nice day," the usual gaff, of course, but I haven't talked a good politics, religion, sex, or taxes in quite a few years.

I must have had a life before I came to Rivas de la Luna twenty years ago, but I have forgotten about it. I remember a blue-white coldness and a chilly feeling of some sort, but only on rainy days, which remind me of something, although I don't quite know what. Chalk it up to imminent senility, if you will. I read an article in my doctor's office about it. It said to take lots of vitamin B-12 and you can reverse the whole process. So I'm working on it. My job pays enough for me to live satisfactorily in my trailer. I do not have a television set, but I do have a typewriter and a cat named "Pip" that sits in the window and waits for me to return each night. I write entries into my daily log at the typewriter. Most of what I write I see from the window on the bus, riding to and from work. This morning, for instance, I saw:

A chunky young man running down the Via Triumphans in the middle of the town. On the back of his tee shirt was written: "No goals, no glory."

A new sign on a billboard that read:
"Unplug coffee.
Feed cat.
Play Lotto."

A white stretch limousine parked in front of the Seven-Eleven.

Two elderly women crossing the street against the light, unaware that three cars were scurrying at their heels wanting to run them over.

A man arriving in a van, jumping out and opening up a store called "The Rug Doctor."

A wooden house burning two blocks away, quite silently, before anybody had yet had time to call the fire department.

Don't ask me what any of these mean. I just put them all together sometimes and call the whole thing a poem. That's the privilege of age--eccentricity. You develop a kind of King Lear logic after a while.

I am one of the regulars who ride the bus. We all know each other and the perils of our shiny plastic seats on the bus. You must sit down first before the driver will start. You cannot stand up when you see your stop approaching.

The three M & M's ride the bus daily. They are Mae, Muriel, and Margaret. I nod to them. I know everything about them. They are willing to tell the whole world their sensational stories. Mae's husband walked out on her when she was thirty. She insists that he was kidnapped by the C.I.A. Muriel is eighty-six, but lies and pretends she's only seventy-two. Margaret, thin and rickety, has hair that miraculously gets redder every year. She went to a fancy private college, but lives in a trailer right near me. She grows geraniums that are the tallest ones I have ever seen.

Christopher Robin rides the bus, also. That is not his real name, but the name I have assigned to him because he has that thin little English whey face. He plays the French horn which he carries with him in a case lashed to a metal luggage carrier that rolls along with him. He is eight years old, and when we reach his stop, his mother and two dogs always put him on the bus. They are faithfully there when he returns, too. The dogs jump up, but Chris jumps down from the bus and gathers them both up in one huge embrace.

Sometimes the wild-eyed religious man gets on. He could be a Greek Orthodox priest, a Russian, or a Coptic something, which is what Margaret claims he is. He has a beard, severely cut, a mean eye, and a curt way of speaking. He wears a black suit with an ominous large cross jangling on his chest. We do not trust him. He sits in splendid, superior isolation by himself.

I occasionally sit in the special seat in front reserved for elderly or disabled persons. My severe arthritis, not to mention my eighty-eight years, makes me eligible for this spot. I have to sit sideways, though, and it is a little hazardous if a certain driver is on. His name is Charley, and he is our cowboy driver. Once, when a red light blinked on in front of him, he cut right through the corner lot in front of a real estate firm to circumvent it. We were all amazed to be riding high on the pavement and to find a clear path ahead. We zoomed down the Via Triumphans like the grand prize winner in some major sweepstakes. But a passenger must have complained, because soon Charley went back to the old molasses way of driving that seems to be preferred. Apparently, there is very little fun or money in driving.

Today, though, Jen is driving. I think we could be in for trouble because I can see it lolling in Jen's eye. There is a slightly wicked look there. She doesn't say much. She's very polite, but we all know she's had a rough life. She has been having difficulty lately with the bosses in the bus company. They have decided that all drivers should rotate their routes every two weeks. This is to prevent burn-out and boredom, so they said. Jen told us that she was one of only two drivers who voted against it. She wants to drive Route One exclusively. That is the route that goes almost the whole length of the Via Triumphans, from the fields outside town, through the center of town, to the university at the other end, after which the road becomes an unknown country way heading north. She has driven this same route for eight years and says she is not about to change. Jen is blonde, blue-eyed, in her forties, and wears lipstick, mascara, and red nail polish. We call her "The Blonde Bomber." She has a pretty face and knows it. Everybody likes her.

Margaret is talking to Jen about her nephew Mark who lives in San Francisco. Jen's mind is not on the subject, but Margaret just presses on anyway.

" . . . says he will come down just for Easter, but I didn't invite him, and, after last time, I don't know that I care to have him running up phone bills and carrying on like that again."

"Jen," interrupted Mae. "Honey, didn't you miss your turn?"

Jen said not a word, and when a passenger in the back pulled the "stop" cord, we ran right on through the stop.

"Let me off here," came a voice from the back.

The bus just sped faster.

"Honey," Mae said. "That man wants to get off."

Muriel burst into tears. "I want to get off," she said to Margaret.

"Stop the bus!" demanded Margaret.

"I rang for you to stop," shouted out the man in the back.

"Sit down, shut up, and hold on!" said Jen.

"Honey," said Mae, pulling out her handkerchief for Muriel, who was in a panic. "Have you lost your fool head, or something?"

"We're going places!" said Jen. Everybody was frozen into instant inarticulation. We flew now through the campus and out the other side. As we whizzed by stops, little groups of students looked astonished at our speed.

Jen headed the bus up the Via Triumphans going north.

"Holy Moley," said a man's voice from the back.

As for my reaction, to tell you the truth, at first I was furious and then I got scared. I thought maybe Jen had been to one of her relatives' smorgasbords she used to tell us about and gotten hold of too much akavit or schnapps, but she seemed in complete control, so I went along with the grand comedy of it all and decided to just kick back and see what was in store for us.

"You off your rocker?" I asked her quietly.

"No," she whispered. "Right on target."

I paused for a minute, considering. "Gun it," I said.

She did and gave me a big smile. I smiled back. I admire a person who goes for it.

"Mr. Willis, is it all right?" said Mae to me tentatively.

"You ever been surfing or skiing?" I replied.

"No."

"Too bad. Same feeling. Exhilarating," I said. "Relax."

So Mae sat back, but I could see her looking at me in sidelong glances and then at Jen to see if we were on something.

We hit the freeway finally, cruising on up toward San Francisco, and Jen settled back with a really sweet, contented smile on her face. Most of the people on the bus were savoring the thrill of irresponsibility by now and were socializing happily, the way you do when you're going on a picnic. Only the priest and a few others were making desperate hand gestures to passing cars, indicating trouble on board, but the motorists ignored them, thinking they were typical California freeway nuts. Well, I thought, she's done it and she's glad. I wonder if she's thought of cops, though?

The clerk at the Marooned Bird Motel argued with Jen. "There's no way I can put up nineteen people."

"Sixteen," interjected Margaret. "That mean priest took off for a telephone booth and those two college students went along with him."

"Sixteen," said Jen to the clerk. "That's eight doubles with twin beds in each."

The clerk checked. "Six, and I'll give you a couple of rollaways. That's the best I can do."

"Done," said Jen. "Now, you just charge all this to the Rivas de la Luna Bus Company."

"I'll need a card," said the clerk.

"They'll send a check," said Jen. "We're on a field trip. Please tell the restaurant there will be sixteen for lunch. We're going down onto the beach a bit."

"May I interrupt?" asked a man from the bus.

"You may not," said Jen. "Leave all your things here. We're going down on the beach. Come on."

"My mother will worry," said Chris.

"We'll call her later," said Jen, putting her arm around him. "Let's have some fun for once in our lives."

"Jen, this is terrible," said Muriel. "I feel as though I'm in some wild adventure."

"I know," said Jen. "Now, you take Mr. Willis by the arm. He's your buddy today. You may have to share a room with him tonight."

Muriel clutched my arm. She giggled foolishly, but at least she had gotten over her tears. Besides, I'd had a hankering for her for years.

"Well, I'll tell you one thing," said Margaret. "We sure got rid of that priest. I've never seen such a sour face."

"Honey," said Mae, catching up with Jen on the way down the staircase to the beach. "You sure got guts."

This beach is a magical beach. It is composed of moonstones and agates. There are delicate shells and beach glass. There are twisted trees, shaped by the winds off the ocean. It is very peaceful sitting here. I like it. It reminds me of something very pleasant and very far away. I am surprised that I can sit down on these smooth round heaps of gems and be comfortable. I don't know whether I shall be able to get up again, but at this point I don't care. I just want to sit here and look out to the sea. I wonder how many miles it is to China? Maybe I ought to travel more to break up the old geriatric routine. Maybe Jen's little sideshow today is a preview of a coming attraction.

But, now, we are trailing after Jen. We are following her back up the wooden staircase to the motel. Chris is telling her about the new song he learned for the French horn. Jan is smiling and relaxed. She is holding Chris by the hand. Mae, Muriel, and Margaret are laughing. Mae is showing Muriel some green beach glass she picked up. Margaret is talking to a college student about Mesopotamian history. The man whose stop was the first one we passed by is walking close behind me and giving me little prods when I need them on the steps.

Suddenly, a large shadow looms at the top of the steps. There are two policemen there and their guns are drawn. We all freeze against the sky.

When the judge said to Jen, "How do you plead?" all fifteen of us rose and said, "Guilty." Our lawyer told us to say that. It was planned.

The judge needed a little recess to think about that one, and when he came back he said he thought he needed to hear a reason from each of us. "Why did you do it?" he asked. Well, we had that one figured out in advance, too, and so each of us was coached to say the same thing when our turn came. We were supposed to say, "We stole the bus because we wanted to see what there was at the end of the Via Triumphans." And everybody did exactly as they were instructed, except me.

I was the last one up to bat. I don't know what came over me. Suddenly, all those years of nobody listening to me just crashed over me like the Pacific Ocean. I spoke up in a clear, strong voice I really hadn't used in years. "Judge," I said. "Your honor. Every so often don't you feel you need to break up the ordinariness of life, take a little holiday to jangle up the old jailhouse routine a bit? That's the way we felt. We're damn tired of being computer chips with social security numbers, zip codes and area codes. So we had a field trip. What's the harm? Probably put a little zip back into the bus-riding business, anyway."

Well, that prune-faced judge did smile a bit, I'll say that for him. He thought I was semi-funny with my Jimmy Stewart telling-off routine, but you know these legal pimps. I could see he wasn't really buying any of it, so I was prepared to be hit with some pretty heavy grief. Actually, the sentence was lighter than we expected. The upshot was Jen, that is, we, got fined $1000, Jen got suspended from driving the bus for two weeks, and we all had to listen to a lecture from the judge on moral responsibility to the profit-making bus company which could be losing money every minute because of some inconsiderate people's whims who went on a joyride. The whole deal wasn't much of a problem to us. We just pooled our money to pay the fine. We all agreed that Jen had suffered enough harrassment and needed a real vacation, so we raised some more money and sent her right on back to the Marooned Bird Motel for three nights on us.

Tomorrow is Monday. The two weeks' suspension are up. Jen's supposed to be on our route again. Mae bought a new dress in honor of her return, Margaret bought some Lanvin's "My Sin" for her, Muriel's bringing her a loaf of home-made bread, Chris has written a song for her, and I wrote a poem. We all wonder if lightning will strike again.

WAY OUT WEST

We couldn't have picked a better night for a celebration of old-time Hollywood than this Paramount dippy-moon night in September. All of us longed to see Oliver Hardy up there on the screen again in this rare revival of *Zenobia*. But then I had to go and spoil it all by pissing blood into the urinal in the men's room. I brought two carloads of people here tonight to have a good time, so I'm not telling them anything they don't need to know. The doctor warned me this would be a sign-off for me, but I figure, what the hell, I'm eighty-five, who gives a damn anyway? We're here for the *Sons of the Desert* meeting and this is my thing, it's what I do, and I want my friends to enjoy themselves tonight.

"Jesus, Junior, will you look at that?" says Howard, grabbing my arm and pointing out a Chevy van like you've never seen before in the parking lot, soldily festooned with brass knicknacks from all walks of life and shining like some glittering solid gold Ben Hur chariot with all traces of its humble General Motors origin hidden.

"That's really special," I reply, taking it all in, including the owner and his wife. I think I recognize them. She's all western, fluffed out hair, cute face, short skirt, latter-day Dale Evans, I'd say. He's a carnival type, dyed black hair, leathery face, stringy, muscular arms covered with tattoos, black shirt and tight pants, turquoise rings, boots, the works.

"Don't I know you?" I ask.

"Probably," the man replies. "Done commercials, chewing tobacco, also one Marlboro once, background stuff. I'm usually atmosphere. Three movies. You ever see *Ranch Raiders Three?*"

"Think I did."

"That was me. The third man. One in black. The murdering dude. Remember?"

"If you saw him, you saw me," pipes up the wife. "I was in that too. The cowgirl with the nice smile. I also did a Red Skelton show on television and was one of the western dancers in a CBS special. What was it called?"

"Something about prairie life," says the husband.

"No. It was called *Arizona Settlers: The Originals*, I think."

"That's it," the husband replies. "Damn good show, too."

"I didn't see that," I apologize.

"Where did you get all this junk?" asks Howard of the carny man, looking pointedly at his armadillo van.

The man frowns. "This is not junk," he snaps. "I was offered $500,000 for it." He points to a brass buckle on the driver's door. "See that? That's Stevie Wonder's brass buckle." He indicates a large Roman coin with a man's face on it. "Bet you can't guess who that is?"

"Frank Sinatra," chimes in Howard's wife, Carol.

The man beams. "Right. You're smart, lady. If Sinatra looks like Julius Caesar to you, it's because I got this when he played Caesar's Palace in Vegas. Eyetalians used to be Romans. Get it?"

"God," Howard blurts out. "Will you look at all those coins?"

"Four thousand Susan B. Anthony dollars," the man says proudly.

Mannie, Joan, and Chuck join us. "Can we take a photo?" Chuck asks the man.

"Sure. We'll assume the pose." He and his wife smile professionally like Roy and Dale and stand close together so you can get a good view of the van too. "Carry my fortune on my back," brags the man, indicating his golden van.

"Much obliged," says Chuck.

"No problem," the man laughs. You know he loves it.

"Let's go stand on line," I suggest because I see some new people gathering by the entrance to the building.

"This is going to be fun," says Carol. "Thank you for bringing us, Junior. I think I'm going to enjoy this evening. It's very unusual."

My treat, I think, but will my friends really like it? Some do, some don't. It's kind of a California aberration, I admit, maybe better for declining dinosaurs like me, a harmless, dumb kind of recreation, like golf or canasta or skateboarding which some people even older than I are stupid enough to try out here in California.

What I worry about primarily is the locale. I think it's typical, but a lot of out-of-towners really want the Beverly Hills stuff, not these flat, sleazy outer reaches of North Hollywood. It's really a disappointing industrial area here on Victory Boulevard. There are long blocks of warehouse-type architecture, tacky little houses when you find them, lousy bus service--and, well, it looks like the early days of Hollywood before it all began. That's why I find it appropriate, I guess. It's the sort of ordinary place Charlie Chaplin and Hal Roach found and then they made something magical out of it, like turning La Brea into Tudor England, the way Chaplin did.

We meet in the Mayflower Club, possibly the least likely place on earth to find a collection of Anglophiles, but that's what it normally is--an Anglo-American club decorated with British flags, framed photos of the Queen, the Queen Mum, Princess Anne, Prince Philip, all those still in favor at the moment, the list gets shorter every day. Then once a month my organization, the *Sons of the Desert* takes over and we have our meeting to which we can bring guests.

If you remember the work of Oliver Hardy and Stan Laurel in the movies then you've got our number precisely. You'll instantly understand what we're up to, why we meet. *Sons of the Desert* was founded in New York in 1964 to perpetuate the memory of Laurel and Hardy. We have many branches, called "tents" throughout the United States. Each tent is named after one of their movies. Los Angeles is known as the *Way Out West* tent, which we shorten to the WOW

Tent. I was one of the founders of this tent. My dad was one of Hal Roach's cameramen, worked on every single one of Hardy's films (including *Zenobia*) and is a celebrity among those in the industry.

The WOW tent meets about every six weeks and we have an annual banquet, usually in October. Typical of all our meetings, including tonight, is a none-too-serious business meeting, a guest speaker, a door prize raffle, and a film or two. Tonight we're going to view *Zenobia*, one of the few films Babe (that's what we call Oliver Hardy) made without Stan.

It's isn't only just selfish adulation. We do some good things, too. We have set up a Laurel and Hardy scholarship fund for promising comedians. We helped put up a commemorative plaque at Babe's grave. We got a park named in honor of Hal Roach in Culver City. Once, for fun, we re-staged the great pie fight from *Battle of the Century*. The WOW Tent also hosted the second International Convention of *Sons of the Desert* in 1980 in Los Angeles. We also publish a newspaper called *Pratfall*, and help other people sets up tents in their communities. We do everything free. There are no paid staff anywhere in the whole organization. We do it out of respect for the boys.

Well, we're early tonight, the first ones here. No, there's one other guy. He's gassing away with some of my guests. I've seen him before. His name is Burris. He fixes you like the Ancient Mariner and buttonholes you with his spiel: "I always come here. I'm seeking out happiness. I don't come to see celebrities. I never attend the banquet. I just want to see the old pictures. I want to see the boys again. I want everybody to be happy. That's why I say this is the happiest place on earth."

Carol looks from him to her husband, rolling her eyes slightly, as though saying, "What have we gotten into?" Then I follow her gaze as she directs it toward the table where Jim Plunkett is setting up his souvenirs. She notices the bumper stickers that say "This is another fine mess you've gotten me into," which make her smile and her gaze indicates to Howard that he should notice them too. Howard picks up a Turkish fez, examines it, starts to put it on his head, causing laughter from our whole group, drops it in amazement when he spots a guest approaching who is dressed like Ollie in short pants with a tiny bowler hat on his head. Howard's quick eye sweeps over the souvenir table, inwardly sneering at all the detritus he sees associated with dead icons.

Martha Rossignol has come into the room now and is setting up her cash box at a cardtable. She smiles at me, says "How're you doing, Junior? You're looking just fine." Lucky she said all that before I could reply because I was feeling a lot of pain in a sensitive area I didn't want to talk with her about. I thought I just wanted to sit down. "I don't need to see your identification. Four guests, is that right?"

"No, six. I phoned in."

"Who'd you talk to? Wasn't me."

" Don't know. Maybe Sam."

"Nope, Sam's in Vegas. Been gone a month."

"Well, somebody."

"Probably Joe Rotherburg. He doesn't write things down."

"That's him. Yeah, it was Joe."

"Let me just make a note," says Martha, writing with her right hand and handing me a bundle of name tags with her left. "There. Just have them write in their own names."

"Thanks."

We go into the hall, take our seats at a table near the bar. More people have filtered in now. I recognize June Lang, who's in *Zenobia*. She is as tall, slim, attractive as ever, still blonde, wears a smart beige suit. Looks more like a top executive than an old-time movie star. She talks with two men at the bar. I take orders from my crowd. Two draught beers, three cokes, one whiskey sour, two ginger ales. Man next to me at the bar clutches an "Another Fine Mess" bumper sticker he bought, maybe the most famous quote from the boys.

Burris shows up at the bar now, says to the man: "Isn't this great? Aren't you happy? Junior is, aren't you?" he says to me. "Junior's daddy was the cinematographer on everything. Babe said he was the best, didn't he? Look at this." His gaze sweeps over the far corners of the room where people are swarming around the souvenir tables. "Turkish fezzes, little bowlers, records, tapes, movie stills, ties, calendars, tee-shirts, bumper stickers--all to honor the boys and their work. Is there any better world? Don't you think so, Junior? Isn't this the happiest place on earth?"

"If you say so, Burris," I reply, taking another load of drinks to my table.

"The whole world should know this," shouts Burris at me. He holds up the man's bumper sticker. "Be proud of this," he says. "May God bless the car that wears this." The man smiles and Burris moves away to deliver his spiel to some newcomers at the door.

After drinks, Don Albert, our current president, stands up and clinks a spoon against his glass. He invites us to move into the folding chairs set up opposite the movie screen. "I want to introduce a few celebrities who are in our midst tonight," he says. We all shift into the seats, I finding them especially uncomfortable with all that metal biting into my back, but I make sure my guests all get center seats so they can see the picture well.

"We're all grateful to Billy Sanderson, who brought in this print of *Zenobia* from his home in Encino," says Don. "*Zenobia* was filmed in 1939, released in 1940. It's really the only full-length feature film Babe ever made without Stan. You'll see Jean Parker, James Ellison, Billie Burke, Alice Brady, June Lang, Harry Langdon, and Zenobia the elephant in it. Now I want to introduce Harry Langdon's widow, Mabel Langdon, who is in the audience tonight."

Mabel stands up, blue print dress, grey hair, glasses. "Well, it will be good to see my husband again," she says. Then she introduces her grandson, baby-faced Harry Langdon III and his kewpie-doll daughter, who sit in the back row. We all applaud vigorously. Mabel tells us that all the exteriors in the film were actually shot on the studio lot. She says we will notice her son, Harry Langdon, Jr., driving the cart in the film.

Next, June Lang is introduced and she recounts that the great actress Alice Brady drank champagne and ate caviar during the making of the picture. June says this was odd, yet charming, since Alice was playing her mother.

Finally, I hear Don say, "And our last celebrity is Junior Caswell, whose father, Herbert Caswell, was a major photographer on most of the Laurel and Hardy films." So I stand up awkwardly, take a bow, give a bit of the royal wave. As I sit back, the lady directly in front of me, turns around and whispers, "I knew you were somebody." I say, "Thank you," as the room darkens, the familiar whirring from the projector starts and the screen lights up with the title and credits. I see right away the light in the projector is inadequate. The film looks more like something from 1912 than 1939.

Zenobia is only mildly amusing. Billie Burke overdoes her tiresome fluttering number, June Lang and Alice Brady are trapped in stereotypical roles, Jean Parker and Jimmy Ellison look attractive, Harry Langdon plays deadpan. Only Babe and the elephant manage to pump some meaning and feeling into the film. Babe is a small town doctor who befriends Zenobia, this great galumphing elephant, imperfect and uncertain as life itself, who provides the few moments of sympathy on the screen. Babe rescues her and Zenobia is so grateful she goes barging into his house in search of him, so that Zenobia becomes an embarrassing presence in his life, something Babe doesn't know how to deal with. I hear Burris chortling happily throughout, but I hear a man behind me saying, "The director stinks. The picture was a disaster from the word 'go.'"

I personally feel ill. I excuse myself to go to the men's room. Nothing has changed. I feel as though I'm sliding downhill with no brakes. I come back and sit down. "You all right?" asks Chuck on one side of me. "Yes," I whisper. Helen, on the other side, pats me reassuringly on the arm, but in another minute I catch her nodding off. The film is so dark and flickering that it looks like the antediluvian beginning of movies. Everybody's attention wanders. Nobody's going to compliment me on Dad's work this time, I can see that.

When the movie is over, we give it scattered applause, Burris standing up like a demented cheerleader, shouting, "Great show. Loved Zenobia. Babe proved he could do it alone. This is the happiest place in the world, isn't it?"

Then Don pops up, stands before the crowd, and says solemnly, "Before we go, folks, let's not forget. Join hands now."

"What for?" asks Helen.

"The anthem," I tell her. "Look at your program." Now we all link hands, swaying as we sing the song from *Sons of the Desert*, the movie Laurel and Hardy made in 1933, directed by William A. Seiter. In this film, regarded as maybe their best, the boys tell their wives they are going to Hawaii for Babe's health, but instead they go to a lodge convention with fun and good times in Chicago. The boat sinks on the return voyage from Hawaii and the boys have to explain to their wives how they arrived back a day earlier than the other survivors from the wreck. "We shiphiked," they say.

"We are the sons of the desert," we all chant with shaky conviction, "Having the time of our lives, Marching along, two thousand strong, Far from our sweethearts and wives." How it hurts me to sing. Wherever Laurel and Hardy fans gather, you will find this song sung commemorating our favorite comedic duo.

It is dark now, the fezzes and bowler hats dip into the night. The golden chevy van pulls out. June Lang exits grandly through the tacky door with its peeling paint. The lights go out on the British royal family on the wall. We move into the hard, real world of Victory Boulevard. I feel the pain in my groin worsen. I know my face is drawn and ashen. I'll call my doctor in the morning. The last thing I see is Burris' face glowing with a great smile on it. "Your Dad did a great job," he says to me. "I thought the filming was beautiful, just beautiful."

"Wasn't it?" I lie. And then I notice the man from the bar attaching his bumper sticker—"Another Fine Mess." I'll worry about that tomorrow, I think, and hurry my guests into their cars, as though Burris's very presence is a threat to them and I an embarrassing Zenobia.

THE GAME ROOM

THIS IS WHAT HE HEARD AT THE MERRILLS' COCKTAIL PARTY ON JENKINS' HILL:

He took a thirty-three percent pay cut so he's looking around."

"Alison's his third wife. I don't think he's a very good doctor."

"We love it in France. Only Gerard bought a second home and that is a no-no. Now we have to pay $250,000 starters if we sell it. So we're going to have to move into this second one, and sell the first one."

"Vermont is so tidy; New Hampshire's so run-down. It suits me perfectly. Is there anything for sale around here, Tom?"

"Joanne is my wife, Janet is my sister. Yes, they do look alike. Does that straighten things out?"

"We were in the navy together. We bought Jean Harlow's car. Howard Hughes had given it to her. It was a 1931 custom-built 16-cylinder Cadillac."

"Of course you don't see him here. Terry had to fire him from the bank."

"Thank you, Tom. You do make a beautiful martini. I hate the desecration that's taken place, just throwing gin on the rocks."

"Well, listen. We're just up the road. Why don't you stop by sometime and we'll show you what he's done."

"You hate Marblehead?"

"Anita's changed so. She looks great. California, did you say?"

"Who is that? The one in the shocking pink jacket."

"He sold them his twenty-year old novel, and that pleases him, but they threw him off the set, so he's not happy with the film."

"Don't I remember you from Mustique? Aren't you David's cousin?"

"I'm one of the notorious Merrills of New Hampshire. My brother is your host."

"Thank you, dear. She's ninety-six. We finally got her into a retirement home. We were all calling her Miss Havisham."

"Buffy's at Vassar. Muffy's at Smith. Didi's at Framingham Community College. She wants to be a physical therapist."

"Isn't the view spectacular? You can see Liberty, Lincoln, and Lafayette. If you go up to Franconia to Robert Frost's place on Ridge Road, you can see exactly the same view from the other side. Isn't that interesting?"

"Is she the one who's got the barn full of oriental stuff from Thailand?"

"Excuse me, I just want to step outside to see the view."

AND THEN HE SAW A LUMPISH BLACK SHAPE MOVING DOWN BY THE HEDGE IN THE MEADOW NEAR THE SIDE OF THE ROAD:

"Hey, Tom, what's that?"

"What?"

"See that black lump down there. I don't have my glasses on."

"God, it's a bear."

"A bear?."

"A black bear. He's after the blackberries."

"Smart bear," said Loris. "I think I'll join him."

"I wouldn't," said Tom. "He'd probably run away anyway. They're basically shy."

"Me, too," said Loris.

Marliese, his wife, joined him. "What are you staring so intently at, darling?"

"A bear. See him down there? Oops, now he's disappeared."

"How many drinks have you had?"

"Just two."

"Don't have anymore. I've invited the Brunels back to the house for dinner. They were in Gstaad last Christmas and New Year's. You'll be surprised at their news."

"Sure," said Loris, sitting on the stone wall at the edge of the terrace. "I like surprises."

Marliese cupped her hand under his chin. "Don't sulk, darling. And don't take another martini."

"They're good, Marliese. Dame Dorothy said he makes them the right way."

"Sh, sh. I know," she winked. "Don't be satirical. Isn't she something?" Marliese went back into the thick of the party in the house, leaving Loris looking off in the distance to where the bear had been.

AFTER THEY DROVE HOME FROM THE PARTY THAT EVENING:

Loris parked the car in the barn, walked with Marliese to the kitchen door of the house, opened it for her, followed her into the house, went to the bathroom, watched as she started setting the table in the dining room, listened to her chitchat about the Merrills and their guests, turned on the television set, snapped it off when he saw Tom Brokaw's familiar face on an NBC news special anouncement, picked up the *Laconia Evening Citizen*, scanned its headlines, threw it down, picked up The *Boston Globe,* same fate, *New York Times*, ditto, decided he'd forgotten something in the car, went out the front door toward the barn, walked past the barn, around the barn, up the road that climbs the hill toward the woods and pond, kept on going into the darkening world, uncertain of what he would do, why he was doing it, who he was, propelled only by a tingling sensation along his spine and the notion that he might meet the bear, also an outsider at a cocktail party over on merry Jenkins' Hill.

He turned and took a last look at the farm. It looked blue and cozy, settling into a dramatic landscape, a yellow glow emanating from the kitchen and dining room windows where he knew Marliese was humming and buzzing as she spun her honey feast for the visiting Brunels. But the familiar was not for him now, only the dangerous and uncertain.

HE WHO WAS ASLEEP IN THE GAME ROOM:

"He's probably fallen asleep in the game room," shouted Marliese. "Just open the door, Eugenie, and see if he's conked out on the couch."

Eugenie Brunel opened the squeaky screen door, turned on the lights which were just three overhead lights rigged in a straight line over the center of an unfinished room that looked like a shed. In the blackish distant corner of the room she made out what looked to be a couch and several overstuffed chairs ranged around a huge circular coffee table. She thought she saw the inert form of Loris curled up in a fetal position on the couch.

"Yes," she called back to the kitchen. "I think he's just sleeping."

"Wake him up," called Marliese. "Tell him dinner is ready."

Eugenie said gently, "Loris, your wife has said dinner is served."

No response. Eugenie closed the screen door behind her, pulled the wooden door to, walked through the hall back to the kitchen, closed that door behind her. She faced a determined Marliese bussing plates, glasses, silverware into the dining room. "He is too fast asleep," she announced. "I think it is better to just let him rest."

"Never mind," said Marliese. "Martinis do that to him. Come in, good people. Gerard, we're ready. Now, if you'll just sit there. Eugenie, you there. I want to hear all about Vence. I can't believe you're going to sell that beautiful, charming house."

STUMBLING TOWARD THE POND:

The pond was actually bulldozed out of a swamp with springs and brooks running into it back in 1965 by Marliese's father who wanted to stock it with trout so that his guests could fish for their own country breakfasts. But Marliese and Loris and Marliese's sister and brother-in-law and their two children all found it much more interesting as an old-fashioned swimming hole for skinny dipping. It was large as ponds go in New Hampshire, about the size of a football field. It was just a little off center in their sixty-seven acre farm, totally secluded, surrounded by tall pine trees with white birches arcing across them, forming graceful reflections in the clear, brown, Swedish-lake-like water. Around the pond in season there was a profusion of flowers, violet clover, yellow black-eyed Susans, little orange Indian paintbrushes, goldenrod, wild asters, blue berries. They imported three truckloads of sand to form a sandy beach and entrance to the pond.

Loris saw the pond through the eyes of a child. At the far end was a great granite rock which he called Plymouth Rock. He would lie on his stomach on the plastic float and sail to the rock on his way exploring the shoreline which he imaginatively called Boston harbor, California, the Coast of Illyria, the Swedish Riviera, the Galapagos Islands, strange ports on a great sea with new lands to discover. The inhabitants of the pond were trout, newts, a painted pond turtle, a civilization of frogs. On the surface there were blue dragonflies zooming and touching down, skimming the surface occasionally. Once a great blue heron landed like a Boeing 747, making a splashy entrance and a dramatic exit. There were also mosquitoes, black flies, heavy bomber bees and deer flies in May and June. But usually after the Fourth of July, the sinister insect population dwindled so that the naked human being had little to worry about.

Loris loved the silky feel of the cold water on his body. He always plunged straight in, never hesitating, sometimes swimming, sometimes floating on his back, seeking out the cold shafts of bracing water from the springs beneath. When he emerged, he would shake himself off like a dog and sink into one of the four lawn chairs he had placed there allowing the warm sun to suck up the glistening drops of water from his body until he was dry again. Then he would often repeat the process, immersion, baptism, cleansing, feeling at one with nature. It was a sensual, revivifying experience that he thought about when he was back in dirty, cluttered, suited-up Boston talking with those who worked with him in computers at IBM.

To set the record straight, he didn't blame IBM or the clones that interfaced, faxed, and maxed out all day. Machines beget machines and some brains are robotic computers; he understood that. Maybe he began with too much of a handicap. In a Harvard-Wellesley world, how can a Plymouth State College graduate compete? He had been the local boy, hired to run the machines on Marliese's father's farm, strong, muscular, useful--nobody except Marliese ever thought he had a mind and something more.

And so he had moved into the New England world of the very well-educated and successful, yet his chief distinction appeared to be that he did fit in, he was accepted. and lauded for what he had to overcome. But that story bored him. There ought to be something more than mere Emersonian self-reliance. Perhaps if they lived in California or France. . ? When the old man died and Marliese and her sister inherited the farm, they kept it as a living monument to their father, very little change permitted, no outside interference. It became their weekend retreat, their summer residence. But in that family circle he was still an intruder and therefore untrustworthy. Marliese, as she grew older, grew more like her parents, provincial and intransigent on certain subjects, while Loris grew more rebellious and reckless.

On this night, with just a trace of moonlight overhead, not the full moon he sometimes swam under, Loris had it in his head to make the break finally. I'm going to do the Thoreau, Gauguin thing is what ran through his mind. He would just move to the pond, live there forever, refusing ever to come back to the main house, building his own shelter, perhaps foraging for his own food. He didn't really know what he would do. He knew only what he wanted to do. It was early August, warm at night, he was fortified with two martinis and so all things were possible. He would have to fend for himself. He was not afraid, just angry at the phoniness that had anesthetized the world, furious with Marliese for dragging him over to Jenkins' Hill for another tiresome cocktail hour with the wealthy Republicans of New Hampshire, "Live free or die," yippee.

Loris collapsed into a lawn chair, listened for a while to the sounds of branches breaking in the forest around him and a few frogs croaking out protests at this human invasion. He thought maybe a wooly bear would come and join him and they could play Pooh and Christopher Robin, but when no bear arrived, he dozed off and fell asleep peacefully.

Marliese brought out the good bottle of Pommard she had been saving for a special occasion and served it with her chicken sauteed in mushrooms and black olives. "Poulet et Pommard," she announced. "I hope you don't mind a red with this?"

"Not at all," said Gerard. "This is very nice of you to do."

"Does he do this often?" asked Eugenie.

"Who? Do what? Oh, you mean Loris?"

"Yes."

"Not often. Don't worry about him. Tell me more about Gstaad."

"It's a tale of three mountains," said Eugenie. "The Eggli, the Windspillen, the Wasserngrat. We skied."

"We weren't even in Gstaad this year," said Gerard. "We stayed in Saanen."

"We booked too late," said Eugenie. "There was nothing at the Palace or Park. The chalets are much too dear for us these days."

"What about the Olden?" asked Marliese.

"No chance," said Eugenie. "They only have a few rooms. You have to book more than a year in advance."

"Did Lamont really shoot that ski instructor?" Marliese leaned in to Eugenie.

"Just like that," said Eugenie. "Lolly was flaunting Rudi--that was his name--and Lamont just took the ski-lift to the top of the Wasserngrat and was waiting there when they came up. Zip. Bang. No more Rudi."

"I just missed it," said Gerard."I was behind them down below. Suddenly the whole lift stopped. We didn't know what happened. They telephoned it down."

"They say the snow just turned blood red where he fell," said Eugenie.

"And Lamont?" asked Marliese.

"Nobody knows. The trial is next month. He's in a Swiss jail. Isn't it terrible?"

"You just never know," said Gerard. "You can't tell what a man will do."

"I just would never think that Lamont would . . . " said Marliese.

"I know," said Eugenie. "You can imagine how it just ruined the season. The Riegelbergers actually cancelled their New Year's party this year."

". . . ever have done something so foolish," finished Marliese.

WHEN THE SUN ROSE NEXT MORNING:

Loris lay warming up in the bright sunshine licking at his body sprawled out in the lawn chair. Loris opened his eyes carefully, watching the strong shafts of pine trees swaying imperceptibly against the black-green forest surrounding the pond. Masts for tall ships, he thought, bound for Asia,

Europe, exotic ports in the Caribbean and South America. He listened to the wind riffling paper leaves in birches, maples, and oaks and watched as delicate pollen and husks floated down through the sunlight, motes to land on him, the ground, and the pond. He marveled at the diamond birds skittering over the water's surface when the wind shifted and the light glittered briefly, dancing and vanishing as it kissed the shore.

The heat felt good. The sun could heal and take away forever the bitter taste of people and parties. Loris shifted, sat up, and clumsily took off his shoes, socks, and all his clothes. He adjusted his chair so that he could lie back comfortably. He scrunched up his shirt into a kind of sash so that he could rest it over his eyes to protect them. He remembered that last night he had made the irrevocable break. He had thrown over the known, rotten world once and for all. He would never go back. That decision having been made, he lay back and fell asleep again. In his dream he became a tall ship rocking gently on a beneficent ocean bound for the coast of China far away. He was acutely aware that the mast, his penis, was yawning tall, arcing toward the sun, seeking a union with the source of heat, light and truth. He realized that everything was held in a terrible balance, in jeopardy, and that he was responsible, but he sailed on blissfully until there was an enormous explosion in which he saw himself taking great pleasure, and then he awoke in imminent danger, like a scared surfer caught in the trough of a great wave heading toward a rough landing on a hard, sandy beach. He lay there, breathing heavily, helpless, for a few moments until he rolled out of the lawn chair, stood up and plunged into the cleansing, cold water of the pond.

After ten minutes, he shook himself off, stood tall and unafraid in the sunlight, wondered whether he were a new man now, reached over to look at his watch, saw that it was 8:07 a.m., pulled on his pants, shirt, socks, and shoes, walked back slowly to the farmhouse, arriving just as Marliese was walking into the kitchen to start the house humming again for a new day. Loris entered through the screen door from the game room.

Marliese took out the orange juice from the refrigerator. She walked over to him to receive her morning kiss. "That wasn't very nice of you," she said.

"What?" he said, holding her slightly and smiling, trying to determine if she knew she had almost lost him forever.

"Crumping out in the game room," she said. "But I forgive you. The Brunels weren't all that interesting."

"Sorry," he said. "You know I don't like that crowd."

"You're right," Marliese said. "But, darling, you don't have to drink so much."

"Well, Tom makes a good martini."

"I know, but it just makes you so unpleasant and sleepy."

"All the better to dream by."

"Nobody has dreams anymore," said Marliese. "Don't you know they're called nightmares now?"

LATER THAT WEEK:

Tom Merrill called. He wanted to know if Loris wanted to fly up to Berlin with him in his Cessna. Loris said yes.

It was a fine New Hampshire day, cobalt blue sky, no clouds; you could see Winnipesaukee, Squam, Newfound lakes clearly. You could pick out Chocorua, Lafayette, and Mt. Washington.

"I'll pass over your farm," said Tom. "Do you want me to buzz Marliese?"

"No," said Loris. "Fly over the woods. I'd like to see what the pond looks like from the air."

"Right." Tom flew down low so that Loris could get a good look. The pond appeared suddenly, looking uncharacteristically deep green and blue, and then it vanished quickly into the dark forest again. The whole landscape looked different from the air.

"An ocean, a pond, a drop," said Loris.

"What?" asked Tom. "Did you see it?"

"I think I saw it," said Loris. He let it go at that.

THE FORT

Written from somewhere very high up. Since the divorce, I now live in the tops of trees overlooking a courtyard with brick buildings on three sides. Maybe I'm a bird or the Holy Ghost. Looks something like the Harvard yard where I went to college. I could be back in my third floor room in Hollis 16 waiting to hear the reassuring sounds of students in the night drifting up to me in my elm tree nest in the sky. Only now I'm Rinehart, that lonely Harvard student, who stood under his dormitory room calling out his own name under cover of darkness so others would think he was popular. Was ever a dying man so sought after?

But the truth is this place only looks like a college campus. It really is a red brick condominium garden community, full of lawyers and government workers, in Virginia outside Washington, D.C. We bought here in 1983 when it seemed perfect, advertised as a gentrified Eden where young women with Clairol blonde hair and tanned limbs played tennis all day long and handsome young executives came home to their yuppie paradises every night in their Saabs and Volvos. People were/are eternally young here, forever beautiful, kind, and polite.

It was easy to buy into this dream. Vilma and I had just racked up four years in Germany where I worked with the army engineers. We had adopted our first child, Konrad, a dark, serious boy whose father had been a U.S. soldier who had abandoned a pregnant German woman. Then, as so often happens, Vilma conceived our second son, Oliver, who was born in Washington just after we moved back. Lars, our third son, was born three years later. He grew up in the garden of Eden. He has never known any other home but this. I asked him once how he liked having Adam and Eve for his parents. He just smiled.

The onco man, whom I go to every week, that genius doctor who knows all the answers for terminal cases like me, says it's good if I write all this down. He says, "Keep a journal, man. It's the best therapy." To ensure that I do, he insists I bring it with me. He critiques and grades it for me.

"Just like a godamned teacher," I say.

"Yeah," he replies. "I figure you need a few lessons."

"Not at fifty-six," I say.

"Oh, yes," he replies. "Don't drink so much. Don't smoke at all."

"Fuck you."

"Write," he says. "I want to see that journal next week same time."

"You got it. But don't push me."

"Consider," he says, "where you are, Swanson."

WHAT I SEE:

The difference between yesterday and today. The two sycamore trees that guard the courtyard down below were a gorgeous burnished gold a few days ago. The autumn was a spectacular one this year. I hoped it would never end. But the wind came up and twisted the magic out of the trees. In just two weeks the weather grew colder and all this biting air blew in from the Arctic via the Midwest. It turned the foliage brown and lifted the huge fan-shaped leaves off the twin sentinels, wrestling them down gracefully to form two great mounds of brown crisps on the greying green earth. I wanted to run down and crunch my way through them the way I did in my youth in Fayetteville, New York, when you could still burn leaves in the gutters and thread your way through the smoldering fires along the street with the smoke filling your nostrils, hair, and clothes, so that you smelled as good as any dinner you might sit down to.

But I don't want to move much anymore. I think it's wiser to conserve my energy. I'm content to sit here and just watch. I have a good window for it. There's just a spartan shade on it, nothing more, to be drawn only when necessary I can't stand curtains. I don't like blinds. I want light. I crave viewing space. I want to see it all.

I learned that you don't have to go far away when you split. Not in this planned community. I bought myself a smaller one-bedroom second floor apartment catty-cornered in the courtyard from where Vilma lives with the boys in our old place I can physically breathe the same air I've been breathing for the past few years. I can walk through my usual space, under familiar trees, see the people I'm used to and those I love, watch the re-runs of my life, knowing that I am not corporeally far away, delaying the day when it all becomes immaterial.

But my new apartment suits me well. I have a spiral staircase that goes up to a loft where a guest could stay, if I ever had a guest, or where I could store my books, which is what I do. My kitchen is small, but functional, and has everything I need. I have room to fix a drink and make a meal. I'm a passable cook. My chili is much sought-after at courtyard parties, once or twice a year. I call the place my Bonivard belvidere apartment because outside my window lies the most beautiful view in the world: my sons, my wife that used to be, the shade of the man I was.

There's a parade of children coming by now, kicking at leaves, heaving books on the ground, rolling, jumping, punching each other on the back and arms, skipping--the choreography of the young, longing to fly, challenging gravity. My kids are among them, only they arrive in a Dodge van, driven by Vilma, who has the constitution of a kindergarten teacher able to do it all. Sometimes they look up at my window to see if I'm watching, looking out for them. They are eight, seven, and four and boast of having two houses in one courtyard. No other kids can claim that. But there is a distance between us now. A circle has been drawn around me, or, rather, I've vanished behind a barrier. It's been my own doing, the onco man says, and I know he's right although it pains me to admit it.

So I can't/don't complain. I like tv dinners now I understand the music of long silences.

I open the window slightly. My boys are just underneath. Helen McCardle's father, who is visiting from Montana, is leaving her apartment My youngest, Lars, is staring at him. "Yar so old," the troll says in a clear voice.

"What?" Helen's father leans on his cane.

"He says, 'You're so old,'" offers Ollie.

"Yar glee and ya woks funny," laughs the troll.

"You're ugly and you walk funny," translates Ollie.

"That's a fine thing to say," I hear the old man retort.

"It's true," Ollie says. I can just see the challenging look in that kid's eyes.

All three boys laugh. The old man shakes his cane at them in mock annoyance. "You shouldn't talk that way," he says, scuttling down the pavement.

"We think you look like Scrooge," Ollie calls after him. I consider shouting down to them to stop, but I figure they are coming up to see me and I'll reprimand them later. I settle back in my chair, straighten up the newspapers lying on the floor around me, wait for my buzzer to ring. It doesn't. I look out the window. They are teasing Fireball, the orange manx cat. She runs under a big pile of fan leaves, looks out at them. They leap in after her. The sound and rustle of leaves animates them all. Kids and animals make games out of the simplest things.

Vilma comes back from the house into which she brought some groceries. She locks the van, looks toward the boys. I draw back into the dark space of my room. I don't like her seeing me watch all the time She calls to the boys: "Ollie, Konrad, Lars. Time to come in now." I know their routine. They will have baths now, wash up, help set the table. Then they will have dinner, homework, and time to play before bed. Maybe they'll come by to see me.

We go into November. I break out the windbreaker, the watch cap, and the sweater, I walk around the courtyard a little each day. I no longer can make my usual long walk in the morning to the supermarket, three blocks away. It is fatiguing. I have lost some weight, although not around the middle. People say I look good, but I reply, patting my stomach, "Why don't I lose any weight here?" Vilma takes my grocery list twice a week and buys food for me. She takes me to see the onco man. Twice she has mentioned a hospice in northern Virginia. I tell her I'm not interested. I can manage. She says I can't and it isn't fair to her. I don't say anything. She's right She works two jobs, translating for the government and teaching at Georgetown. I'm the one that's wrong What can I say?

Odd that we should end up like this, Vilma in charge. It was the other way around when we met in Munich. She was German, had just graduated from the university and was translating for the U.S. Army. I was working for the army corps of engineers on a big project in Heilbronn. She helped me write up our proposals and specs. She speaks five languages, English, German, French, Italian, Spanish. She has a large technical vocabulary, is a whiz on a computer. She's fifteen years younger than I. I was flattered that she was interested in me. She showed me Munich. She took me to Vienna, educated me in Mozart and Schubert. We went skiing in Kitzbuehl and Gstaad. I had already divorced my first wife. Vilma had never been married. She told me I was the first man she had really loved. I was surprised We were married in her hometown, Wasserburg, just outside Munich. Her grandmother, who had survived World War II, was thrilled. Vilma had reddish hair, pale skin with some potato chip freckles, and frank blue eyes. She listened carefully to everything I said. Her replies were always sensitive, intelligent. She told me I was everything she wanted in a man. I couldn't believe my luck. And so we got married, sure of a future. She was always optimistic, certain there was more happiness ahead. I was cautious, but she drew me along with her on her positive tide. She wanted a child right away, but we had trouble conceiving. An army doctor suggested adoption. It was easy to do at that time. Konrad was our choice. In three months, Vilma was pregnant. Oliver was born just after we returned to Washington. Then we moved here, where Lars was born in Alexandria a couple of years later.

There are blank spaces now, lacunae in my life which I don't care to write about, especially when the onco man is looking. He knows what I'm talking about. He knows me, knows the symptoms. I'm past talking now. I'm an old man with night sweats, a hacking cough and a pre-determined destiny now. I'm to be a statistic, a number, a fitting conclusion for an engineer, I feel. Vilma has talked with the good doctor, too. I don't know what he's told her, but it's broken us off for good. One of us is drowning. The other is swimming boldly and beautifully, as usual.

Today is November 13th, as if counting days matters. The piles of leaves beneath my window have been made into three great mounds of shifting leaf huts. Yesterday, I stood outside and shouted commands at my boys: "Hey, you, Konrad, build that house of leaves up higher. You can't jump into it like that. Lars, throw the blanket on the leaves. That'll hold them down. Oliver, don't bring the dog into the leaves with you. He'll shake them all over the house."

"Aw, Dad, he won't."

"Don't put the blanket on the dog, Lars. He'll grab it."

"He loves it, Dad. He's having fun."

I gave up. They were having fun. So was I. The air had a sting to it, the promise of winter with the cold kiss of snow to come. Exhilarating.

Konrad ran into his mother's house, came out with a large cardboard box He clapped it over Murgatroyd, our English springer spaniel. Murgatroyd obliged by sliding along with it. It looked as though the box were moving on its own. A Marx Brothers routine right in our own front yard. This set off screams of laughter from Lars and two of his friends who had joined in the action. Ollie ran after the box, beating it with a stick.

"Don't do that, Oliver," I yelled. "You'll scare the dog."

"It's just a game, Dad," said Oliver. "Can't you understand anything?"'

I thought everything was just fine. What would you expect me to say? I knew I was a prisoner, but I was close to where I wanted to be.   Who isn't imprisoned in something, somewhere? Maybe I was a caged bird, but I wasn't obliged to sing anymore. It wasn't expected. I was protected, privileged even, insulated, yet isolated, that was the worst part of it. Wasn't it like being on a desert island with the books you wanted? Few are ever so lucky.

I didn't really go through the typical denial, anger, resignation, acceptance cycle. My training has taught me to stick to the moment, to the facts in front of me. I hate making a fuss over things. I have, perhaps, a scientist's interest in dispassionately watching things happen to me. I remember a professor whose course I took at Rensselaer. He happened to be teaching philosophy and he burned his hand on a stove. He reported it objectively as though it had been a beautiful philosophical experience. We all thought he was nuts at the time, but I always admired his attitude. Now I'm at that place. That was the best course I took.

I think I was a good engineer for many years. I worked on three bridges in Europe, an army base in Spain, and the Bridge of the Americas linking Central with South America. I was proudest of that, I guess. It was an extension of the Panama Canal, the greatest engineering feat ever, in my estimation. My longest stay was five years in the Philippines at Clark. I liked the islands, but the politics was something else. I saw lots of graft, corruption. People were ripping off each other to the right and left. That gets to you. That's when I slipped into alcoholism and began the great decline. The onco man tells me now, " Quit, cut down." What's the point?

I think I was a fool, that's all.

December 21st:

It began snowing last night. You could hear the dull thudding of it on the roof all through the night. A bluish light flickered in all the windows. Steve, the nurse, turned off the light I left on about an hour after he thought I had fallen asleep. He stays up in the loft. At first I resented him, but I need round-the-clock help now. I cannot do everything for myself. He plays cards with me, sometimes reads the newspapers aloud. We watch television, like the same shows, follow the Redskins, so that it works out okay.

Below, on the Rialto, not everyone is stirring. Some cars cannot get out of the parking lot. Carol Corliss' Volkswagen won't start. She gives up, walks over to the bus stop. I guess it's really cold. Carol's breath makes a little puff in front of her face.

It's 4:00 p.m. now. Steve is out shopping. He had to walk. I wanted real coffee. I hate Taster's Choice. I demanded bacon and eggs for breakfast tomorrow. We had an argument about that. He'd better show up with them or I won't let him in the door. I can bolt it. I have an extra chain I've never used.

My little trolls are out on the snowy lawn playing with their friends. Murgatroyd is with them. That springer spaniel is like one big kid. He has to be in on everything they do. He pokes his nose into the middle of their play. They are building a large circular fort, it appears. It is quite an enterprise. They have piled it up good and deep, about three feet, I'd say, and they have packed it down and patted it into perfection. As the three of them go inside, they disappear from view whenever they move close to the wall nearest my apartment. They should put a roof on it, but they don't seem to think it needs one. Their friends stand around, watching. Maybe they intend to have a big snowball fight with their playmates and use this as their refuge.

Now they have brought Murgatyroyd into the fort. He looks goofy. All you can see is his long snout scanning the horizon looking for errant squirrels or Fireball and other cats. It is like a silent movie—my boys, all pink faces and running noses, one mitten on, one off, watchcaps and hoods, and Murgatroyd nosing his way among them, Beau Gestes in their Foreign Legion stronghold waiting for the attack.

Out of the swirling snow, I see Steve arrive. He carries two paper bags. He stops to talk to the boys. I can't hear what he's saying. But I see all three turn and look up to my window for a moment. I wave to them, but I don't think they can see me. The storm window is frosted too much. I see them as in a Monet painting, very distant, very blurred.

It has been snowing all this evening. It makes me jumpy. I worry about snow accumulating on the roof, caving in, knocking us all to hell. I can't sleep. I lie awake waiting for daylight. I dread the blueness of the night. I keep a light burning on the table to remind me of sunlight. I write a few sentences in the journal for the good doctor.

I doze off occasionally into a kind of limbo. I dream of hearing a telephone call, a ring of the buzzer.

I try to sort out the unfamiliar faces that float before me.

I wonder if anyone will come to see me today.

Roger Lee Kenvin is the author of three collections of short
stories and a play published in India. He was educated at
Colgate, Bowdoin, Harvard, and Yale and makes his home in
California and New Hampshire.